PURR FOR ME : BAD BOY AUTOS

Drive Me Wild #2

BRONWEN EVANS

PURR FOR ME
DRIVE ME WILD—Bad Boy Autos

Published By Bronwen Evans 2020

This book, *Purr For Me*, is a work of fiction. Names, characters, places, and incidents either are the product of the author's imagination or are used fictitiously. Any resemblance to actual persons, living or dead, events, or locales is entirely coincidental.

Copy Editor: Leigh Kaye
Cover: Les

Purr For Me...

From USA Today Bestselling Author, Bronwen Evans, comes her latest sexy contemporary romance! A forbidden romance with her ex's elder brother set in Bad Boy Autos. Think Fast and Furious but nothing illegal!

Lexie (Lex) Walker owes her boss, Tom Lorde everything. When her loser husband ran off with her money, she needed to find a job and quickly. Tom took her in and hired Bad Boy Autos first female mechanic. So she can hardly say no when he asks her to work on Kade Colter's car, even when every nerve-ending in her body screams to run. Falling for one Colter was stupid. Falling for his older brother would be a whole lot of dangerous and stupid in the extreme. She refuses to be like her mother and make mistake after mistake, falling for the wrong type of men.

Kade Colter always goes after what he wants. Only once in his life did he back off, when his younger brother brought home his fiancée, Lexie Walker. Now Jason's gone and there's nothing stopping Kade going after what he's desired all these years. He calls in a favor and soon he's got Lexie working under his hood. He'll take his time, treat her like a princess, and show her he's nothing like Jason. However, slow and careful turns to heat and lust the minute she gets close. He needs to ease off the pedal so to speak, if he's to convince Lexie she married the wrong brother.

Click here to sign up to Bron's Book Club newsletter and receive your FREE eBook.

Read other books by Bronwen Evans

Make sure to check out these titles and more on Bron's website.

Chapter One

"You've got to be kidding." Lexie glared at her best friend Tom Lorde as she sat on the other side of his desk in the office of Bad Boy Autos. "I can't believe you're doing this to me."

Tom's returning stare was just as direct. "I'm not doing anything to you. You're the best restorer of Italian motorcars here, and that's what this job needs. Besides, Sully is all over this. Do you really think I'd leave you facing this alone? Sully has your back."

Stay cool, don't get angry.

The private investigator she wanted to hire to find her husband—soon-to-be ex-husband, if she could find Jason—cost more than she ever imagined, and Bad Boy Autos paid the most. She needed this job. Besides, Tom had promised to help her find her ex.

Time was running out. If she didn't find him, and soon, she'd lose... She refused to go there. The very idea made the locket hanging against the bare skin of her neck feel as if it burned.

Lexie lowered her voice to an ominous timber. "That's not what I'm talking about. Kade Colter, Tom. *Kade.* He's my ex-husband's brother. You know, my cokehead husband who cheated on me, abused me, and stole all my money and worse," she took a deep breath, trying to keeping the pain at bay, "he secretly mortgaged my cabin and now I might lose it." Tears filled her eyes.

Nine months ago she'd walked out of her marriage when she'd caught her husband, Jason, in bed with a track bunny. He'd already sold their car and spent the money on drugs, but she'd had no idea that he'd taken a mortgage out on her cabin by forging her signature. He'd changed the address for the correspondence and she'd only learned about it when the person who owned the neighboring cabin rang her to ask if he could buy it. He'd seen the mortgagee sale sign. She had less than three weeks to find the money or she'd lose the cabin. She knew looking for Jason was a waste of time. He'd likely have sniffed the money up his nose, but she would have her divorce and she also might bring charges against him.

Guilt and remorse flickered in Tom's blue eyes before his expression hardened. "I know Jason was a real bastard to you, but Kade always treated you decent, right? They're so different, I can't believe they have the same parents. Besides, a few months ago we turned his business away for you. We can't do it again. Kade could really damage our reputation if he lets everyone know. Never piss off a freelance journalist, especially when he's also a hotshot *New York Times* author. He's the Rick Castle of the racing car world. He's rich and he mixes in the right circles to destroy us."

Sometimes, Tom could be a real hard-ass. There was no point in wasting her breath with her boss, but she didn't have to pretend to like it. She rose and left the office without another word.

"Lexie! Come back here!"

Ignoring Tom, Lexie headed for the bay she shared with Jake Sullivan, aka, Sully. Since he was working on a vintage Indian motorcycle that week, there was plenty of room for the sports car currently parked in the bay—with Kade bloody Colter, leaning against a seen-better-days 1962 Alfa Romeo Spider. The quintessential sports car was a wreck, but it was a pure diamond in the rough.

She caught a quick breath at the sight of Kade before turning her attention to the lone Alfa. It sat there, looking forlorn with its faded and chipped racing red paint. A few scratches ran down the door on the side facing her. They reminded Lexie of the deep wounds gouged in her heart.

She wanted to hug the car; it was damaged like her, but hell, with some tender loving care, it would blossom. She took a gulp of air and rubbed her chest. All it needed was a bit of love. Just like her.

No. Never again.

Love sucked. Like this battered car, she'd become bitter and broken and thrown away.

"Can this morning get any worse?" she softly said to herself through gritted teeth. As she took in the self-assured, handsome as sin Kade. Sweat dripped down her brow as the thermometer inched up to 92 degrees, her temper rising with the mercury.

What a beauty!

She raked her gaze over Kade. Yep, a real beauty. Damn it.

Kade grinned, all denim and swagger, smelling like a male model. Looking like a male model. Hot. She ground her teeth. Handsome wasn't even his middle name. It should be his first— Handsome Colter. And how like him to own the one car her hands itched to work on.

She walked nearer, pushing her hair back off her face. All the better to see the car with—yeah, right? Her gaze shifted from the car to Kade's dark, mesmerizing eyes. He stepped closer, and suddenly the air fled from her lungs. She caught her bottom lip between her teeth to distract him from seeing the pulse pounding hard in the hollow of her throat. Could he see? *Dear God, please no.*

Why had she married the wrong brother? Her life would have been completely different if she'd met Kade first.

She blamed him for making her think that. She'd made her bed and now she was both lying in it, and drowning. She did blame him for the time it took him to decide to help her find Jason. Nine months! It took the letter from the bank saying she was about to lose her property for him to decide perhaps he should share what he knew of his brother's whereabouts. Only now it was too late. Neither of them could find him.

Now she blamed him for insisting she work on his car when she wanted to put the past behind her and pay off all the debts Jason had left her drowning in. She knew it wasn't fair on Kade. Tom was right, he was a decent guy. But she'd asked him to help her find Jason, and he hadn't been very forthcoming. He'd only agreed to help when he learned she could have Jason's ass thrown in jail for fraud. Too little, too late. Was he hiding his brother because she could get him in trouble with the police? She couldn't blame him for wanting to protect his brother. But it didn't mean she had to like him for it.

"I brought you a present." He nodded his head at the Alfa. "How d'you like to work on my car?" Kade's sexy voice added to the headache building behind her eyes.

Placing her hands on her hips, she smiled. Rock and a hard place. Trapped. She could tell him to fuck off, but as her fingers trailed over the chassis, she admitted she wanted this job. Her eyes flashed to Kade. For the joy of restoring the car. Only the car.

A memory of the ATM swallowing her card this morning was all it took to remind her she couldn't afford to lose this job.

Kade stepped closer, and he smelled delicious.

She should run, leave, but Kade's brother had taken all her choices—taken everything, in fact. Money, house, and her pride. The other owner of Bad Boy Autos, Marcus Black, only needed one little reason to show her the door, and pissing off Kade was a big reason.

Her eyes narrowed as she took in Kade's stance, leaning over the hood of the Alfa as if he owned this workshop, with a smug look on that handsome face.

When did she really ever have a choice?

"She'll be amazing when I've finished with her." Her stare dared him to disagree.

"I know," he said as he pushed off the car. "Good—"

"So, what's her story?" Lexie interrupted. The pleasantries were over. She wanted him gone. She started looking the car over. The hood was in the same sorry state as the passenger side. "Needs a complete new paint job but let's see what's under this battered hood. Keys." She held her hand out to Kade.

He gave her a smile that brought back a lot of memories she wished could be excised from her brain. "You haven't changed. Still beautiful when you're pissed off."

She looked at Kade. "I know you're not to blame for your brother's sins, but I can't deal with you at the moment. I have more to worry about than upsetting Jason's brother. So the keys, please."

"I really don't know where he is."

She nodded. "So you've said. Keys. Please."

The warmth in Kade's eyes faded along with his smile. "Look, I know Jason—"

"You don't know shit, Kade, and I'm not discussing anything except this car with you," Lexie said.

Or perhaps not. She eyed Kade, and a risky idea swarmed like buzzing bees in her head. Could Kade lead her to Jason? He'd said he didn't know where his brother was. Her eyes narrowed as she waited for him to hand her the keys. Was he lying? Was he protecting his brother?

Only her pride stopped her from asking Kade to cover the debts his brother had left her with. This was all her fault for being stupid and gullible, so she would fix it. She eyed him slyly. But it wouldn't hurt to have a backup plan. If the worst should happen…

Kade slid his Ray-Bans back on and held out a key ring. She

took it and went around to the driver's side. As she slid into the driver's seat, Lexie spotted Tom standing right behind where she'd just been. His eyes held a steely glint, and he'd crossed his arms over his chest. Their gazes clashed for a moment before she cranked the engine to life.

She smiled at the deep growl that met her ears, but a moment later, the motor coughed, sputtered, and died. Lexie found the release lever and popped the hood. Kade beat her to the punch and had the hood propped open before she'd shut the driver's door.

"It's a mess," Kade said. "Which is why I had it towed here. Bad Boy Autos is the best at this work. Money's no object."

Tell that to someone who didn't know where her next meal was coming from. Her bloody attorney had taken her last two hundred, just so he could tell her that getting any money out of Jason was pretty much a lost cause since he seemed to have fallen off the face of the earth. If only she could afford a P.I.

Her worthless ex took off and left her with debts she could never repay. He'd put the thing she cherished most in this world in jeopardy. She knew she would lose the cabin. She knew deep down inside that even if she found Jason in time, the money would be gone. It had been over nine months since he'd taken out the money, yet she only learned of it a week ago. Fraud was a word that struck like an ice dagger in her heart. He'd fraudulently signed her name on mortgage papers. Hidden his deceit really well by changing the address on the account.

Jason. Just his name made her stomach fill with acid. Handsome, confident, with a sexy-as-sin smile and money to burn, could turn any woman's head. But unlike what she did with cars —i.e., check under the hood—Lexie was too young, too desperate for love, and too stupid to look below his surface.

She didn't want to look under another Colter's hood unless it had four wheels, so Kade could take that come-to-bed smile and try it on a woman stupider than her. But she wasn't opposed to using him to get her property back.

Because you're a reminder of how he ripped her heart out.

Kade told his inner voice to shut the fuck up.

He took a deep breath and noticed Tom staring at him. The message in his eyes said he'd better watch himself around Lexie. Hurting her was the last thing he wanted to do. His brother had hurt her enough. She'd explained Jason was the person who owed her, and she'd collect from him. What churned his gut like a concrete mixer was thinking about what she'd do to Jason if the money was gone. She could have his brother thrown in jail.

Didn't she know she held all the cards? It amazed him Jason's ass wasn't in jail already. He'd fraudulently stolen from her.

Unintimidated, Kade gave Tom a half-smile and lowered his eyes to the car again.

Funny that both of them had the same goal. He wanted to find Jason as much as Lexie did. His bother might be the lowest of the low, but he was still his brother, and he wanted to help him. He'd pay for rehab and hope that Jason stuck at it this time. If Jason refused... then he knew his brother would likely be dead within two years, and he'd promised their mother, on her deathbed, that he'd look after his younger brother.

Guilt. You feel guilty.

He pushed the inner voice away, but he felt guilt... because he'd wanted his brother's fiancée the minute he'd met Lexie, and then she'd married his brother, and a part of him had wanted the marriage to fail—but not like this.

The concentration on Lexie's face fascinated and amused him. It was as though she had X-ray eyes and could see inside the metal, wires, and plastic to diagnose the problem.

"Where d'you get this?"

Her voice startled him a little because he hadn't been expecting her to speak. "From someone I used to know."

Lexie shook her head and put her hands on her hips. "Good thing you have money to burn because this heap of junk will cost a fortune to fix." She pointed out corroded battery terminals, bare wires, and worn hoses. "And that's just what I can see. I have a hunch that when I get it up on a lift, I'll find tons of other stuff wrong with it." Her eyes met his. "Sure you don't want to just junk it and cut your losses?"

Kade responded to the hope in her expression with a shake of his head. "Not a chance. This'll be a sweet ride once you work your magic on it."

"There are plenty of places that could work magic with it."

The right side of his mouth lifted in a half-smile. "Not like you can, Lex. You've got the Midas touch. I'm sure you'll have her purring for me in no time."

Lexie's expression tightened, and she gave a curt nod. "I'll go over her today and work up an estimate of what she needs. I need to get changed so I can get started."

As she walked away, Kade couldn't keep his eyes averted from her fine ass. He tamped down his annoyance over her cold-shoulder treatment, telling himself that it was understandable. Why would she trust a Colter?

"Sorry about that."

Kade shrugged as Tom walked over to him. "No problem. I expected as much."

Tom frowned. "I'll talk to her. Her history with your brother has nothing to do with you, and I don't want it to interfere with our business. Do you know where that loser brother of yours is? That would help her."

"Don't go there, Tom. It'll only make things worse," Kade objected. "I'll find him."

Tom gave Kade a measuring look and nodded. "Okay."

Kade held out a hand to Tom. "It's good to see you again. Let me know how much this will rock me."

"You bet."

After saying goodbye to everyone, Kade got in his silver Mercedes GT and started it. Driving away, he tried to put the scene with Lexie out of his mind, but he couldn't shake the image of the anger and hurt in her eyes. Once again, he mentally cursed his brother for fucking up, but this time was different.

Jason hadn't just given in to his addiction, he'd screwed over an incredible woman like Lexie, and Kade wanted to kick his little brother's teeth in for hurting her so badly—if he could find him.

He might be a freelance investigative journalist, but he hadn't fooled himself into thinking he could do this alone. The private detective he'd hired usually helped investigate any piece he was working on. In fact, he had him on a piece right now.

He was also the one who'd uncovered just how bad Jason's addiction had gotten and the illegal shit he'd done. Nine months ago, he'd fraudulently mortgaged Lexie's cabin and had absconded with the money.

That's the reason he'd insisted on Lexie working on his car. He wanted to talk her into letting him give her the money to pay the mortgage, so she didn't press charges against Jason and have his ass thrown in jail. The money for her cabin and Jason did not get arrested. He still couldn't understand why she hadn't gone to the cops already.

She couldn't possibly still have feelings for Jason?

Well, it wasn't the only reason he'd picked her. She was hot, and he still wanted her.

The idea of her still having feelings for Jason made his chest ache. He'd always had a thing for Lexie, and he wasn't deluding himself. There had been a spark between them, but he wasn't the type to make a move on someone else's woman, especially one his brother wanted to marry. So he'd never acted on that spark.

If she'd been single, would he have made a move?

She wasn't his normal type. So sue him; models were a draw card, and he met plenty in his line of work. Magazine journalists were magnets for models looking to get a foot in the door.

While Lexie was hot, a model she wasn't, but she was still as sexy as sin. Lexie could model in a fitness magazine. She had a body full of sinewy muscles and not an ounce of fat on her.

He smiled. And she had a vicious tongue. He'd never gotten her out of his head. She intrigued and excited him.

For now, he wanted to help her out of the mess his brother had landed her in and save Jason from himself. He admired her resolve to sort it out on her own. Most women he knew wanted his money, usually as much, if not more, than they wanted him. Lexie didn't give a shit about his money, and that was another very attractive quality.

As he downshifted and turned a corner, the little devil on his shoulder laughed. He wanted her, and when in his life had he ever let something he wanted slip away? He just wasn't sure *what* he wanted from the dark beauty. He certainly didn't want to hurt her, and she was still the walking wounded. He'd have to handle Lexie with kid gloves and go slow. Making friends with her was a good way to start out.

The absurdness of his thoughts made Kade laugh out loud. When could they ever be friends?

He must be insane to even consider his plan. Lexie would probably see right through it. He wasn't above offering her the money to save her cabin in exchange for never filing charges against Jason. He wondered if it would be better for Jason to make him face charges. It might straighten him out.

Then his mother's final words played in his head. "He's not strong like you. I overindulged him. Promise me you'll look out for Jason."

Keeping Lexie on his side so she wouldn't bring charges would take all his negotiation skills. Despite that, he was looking forward to spending time with her very much.

Smiling at his reflection in the rearview mirror, he said, "Colter, you're one crazy son of a bitch."

Chapter Two

Lexie looked up when Sully sat down in the patio chair next to her.

He draped an arm along the back of her chair and smiled. "You okay, kid?"

Lexie chuckled and shook her head. Sully was the only person who could get away with calling her "kid." In his mid-forties, he was the oldest person at Bad Boy Autos and was regarded as a surrogate big brother to the crew, the owners included.

"I'm fine." Why ruin the night by sharing her problems?

She took a swig of cold beer and looked out over Sully's huge pool. Crystalline water rippled and sloshed against the sides as several people swam and splashed around. Laughter and '80s rock filled the air. The happy sounds should've lifted Lexie's spirits, but they had the opposite effect.

"Bullshit. You oughta know by now I can tell when you're lying, Lex."

Lexie took another swallow of beer and sighed. "Yeah. It's pretty damn annoying how perceptive you are. Sometimes I just want to keep my feelings to myself, okay?"

Years of being in foster care while her mother beat her addiction taught her it was often better to stay invisible. A problem shared was not a problem halved, because people used you. Used your vulnerabilities.

Sully grunted and propped an ankle on the opposite knee. "You do too much of that."

"What are you? My therapist?"

Lifting a black eyebrow at her grouchy response, Sully said, "Maybe you need one. I know you're trying to find Jason, and why is Kade so insistent about you working on his car?"

"It had crossed my mind too about why me to work on Kade's car." She had a brain. Kade was worried, and so he should be. What Jason had done was fraudulent. She'd never have taken out a mortgage on her cabin, but what Kade didn't understand was proving that fact would cost her money— money she didn't have. If she could just find Jason and get the money back, or what was left of it… she lived in naïve hope. Or at least get him to sign the divorce papers and get him out of her life.

While she was angry and heartbroken, she didn't want to see Jason in prison. Addiction made people into strangers. Her mother had been an addict for most of Lexie's childhood. All she'd needed was help. That one person who didn't give up on her.

Perhaps that's why Lexie stayed with Jason for so long. She thought she could help him.

As her mother had said, "you can't help an addict unless they want to be helped." Jason obviously didn't think he'd hit rock bottom yet.

Only he had, and now she had a decision to make. Turn him in or find him, get the money back if there any, and somehow make him see that rehab was his salvation.

Grinding her teeth together, Lexie tried to bring her anger under control.

Sully was trying to be a good friend, but Lexie was like a

wounded animal. She just wanted to be left alone in her misery to lick her wounds. "I can handle Kade."

"I'm sure you can. And you made it clear how pissed you are at Tom. I'm gonna start calling you the Ice Queen. You froze him out but good."

"Damn straight. He deserves it. Tom knows I don't want a damn thing to do with the Colters." Lexie's hand tightened around the neck of the bottle. "I know Tom thinks he's helping me. He thinks I'll let Kade give me the money if I'm around him enough."

"Well, Kade would you know that." Sully gave her shoulder a squeeze. "It's just business. Colter has a lot of influence. His magazine could really do a number on the firm. Turning him down twice before—well, Marcus and Tom don't need their reputations battered."

"I don't think Kade would do that to Tom. I grudgingly admit he's not as bad as Jason. What I can't understand is, why Kade wants me working on his car?"

"Yes, you do."

She swallowed. "Kade's is looking out for his brother. Tom wants me to forgive Jason so I can move on. I'm not sure I can do that. Tom's expecting too much from me."

"Honey, it's not like that. Kade requested you for this job, and the customer is always right. Besides, Italian motors are your thing."

"Fine, but I won't let him sway me where Jason is concerned."

"I think he already knows that. Just get the job done and Kade will be out of your hair," Sully told her. "Although, I heard Kade offered to cover Jason's debts. A smart girl like you should think about taking him up on his offer."

"Right. Then I'd owe another Colter. It's not Kade's job to clean up his little brother's messes. I don't feel right taking money from Kade. It would make me beholden to him, and I want the

Colters out of my life." Lexie sighed again, wishing Sully would drop the topic of the Colters. "I need to get drunk and get laid." She tossed Sully a wicked smile. "Want to volunteer for the job?"

Sully threw his head back and erupted in laughter. It echoed off his house, and Lexie couldn't resist laughing with him. At least the topic was dropped.

When his mirth had subsided sufficiently, Sully said, "I appreciate the offer, but no. You're gorgeous, honey, but just not my type."

Lexie's shoulders slumped as she feigned disappointment. "I guess I'll just have to settle for getting drunk then."

Casting his eye over the crowd gathered around the pool, Sully grunted. "I'm sure all these other guys would line up for a crack at you."

Gazing around Sully's guests of race car drivers, mechanics and car enthusiasts, Lexie admitted that there was a lot of male eye candy present, and they might have some info about Jason. "What a great idea."

"Okay, but don't get totally blitzed," Sully warned. "Don't need you having a hangover tomorrow."

Lexie barely registered his statement as she watched a couple who were all over each other on the far side of Sully's yard. Their tight embrace and passionate kissing brought tears to Lexie's eyes, as memories of how she and Jason had acted like that when they'd first gotten together flashed through her mind. She'd thought they'd been so in love, and Lexie still didn't understand what had happened between them.

Liar. Cocaine. Boozing. Jason was addicted to both. Why hadn't she read the signs? Perhaps she'd been too young when it had happened to her mum. Or was she simply repeating her mother's mistakes? Men with problems. They drew her mother like a bee to flowers. Plus, Tom had tried to warn her, but she didn't want to listen.

Averting her eyes, Lexie finished her beer. "Thanks for the drink and company, Sully. I'll see you tomorrow."

"Anytime, Lex. If you want some advice, speak to Pace Masters. He's a good guy."

Glancing back at the couple, Lexie said, "Yeah, I could do with some nice guy right now."

"You won't get an argument from me."

She rose and made her way over to where the "boys" were standing by the grill. Most of them she knew from her time working on the European race circuit.

"Hi, Lexie. Long time no see."

She smiled at Pace and nodded. "Hello, boys. Behaving, I hope."

There was a general chuckle. "Not usually," Dave Chester added.

"I heard you're working at Bad Boy Autos. If you ever feel like coming back to the circuit, I'll always have a job for you."

"Thanks, Pace, that's so nice, but my days working with racers are over."

"Yeah, I heard about you and Jason. What a jerk."

The boys all agreed with Simon Walker's words, and she tried to keep a smile on her face.

"You're better off without him. Way too good for the likes of Jason Colter."

She hoped she didn't have to listen to this all night. Just ask the questions and get it over with. She didn't know how long she could hold it together. "Yip. I really can pick them, can't I? Now the bastard's disappeared and I'm trying to find him. Divorce papers, you know."

Pace frowned. "Come to think of it, I haven't seen him around for a while. Have you guys seen him?"

Most of the men shook their heads, except Simon. "I saw him a while back. Said he was heading to the NASCAR Cup in Michigan."

Every muscle in her body went ridged as she fought to keep from showing how important this information was. She could pass this on to a friend working at NASCAR. Perhaps Jason was following the circuit. She swallowed down the excitement because Jason could have lied to Simon.

Since NASCAR was mentioned, the conversation soon turned to racing, and she was about to slip away when Pace reached out and took her hand. "It's nice to see you, Lex. You look really good. I know you're probably not looking for anything serious but if you'd like to have dinner with me one night, it would be my pleasure."

"I'd like that." And as she gazed into Pace's handsome face, she meant it. She'd walked out on Jason nine months ago but their marriage had been over about a year before that. It was time to move on. That's why she wanted her divorce. She held out her phone to share numbers. "Call me."

"You can count on it."

Striding away from him, Lexie barely recognized the hum inside as happiness.

She almost skipped up the driveway to where her tricked-out Jeep Eagle was parked. Driving away from her friend's large place back to her studio apartment hovel, Lexie, for the first time in a while, had something to look forward to.

She pressed dial on her hands-free phone. "Kevin, I've got a lead. I learned Jason said he was going to the NASCAR Cup in Michigan."

"That *is* good work, but I beat you to it. I found a rental car company he used and yip, he dropped it off in Michigan. I'm already here on the ground. Hopefully, I'll have news soon."

No sooner than she'd hung up from Kevin, the detective she'd hired, her phone tinged.

She couldn't read the text until she'd arrived home.

How's dinner Tuesday night? Pick you up from Bad Boy Autos at seven – emoji wink, Pace.

She hugged herself all the way into the house, but the happiness died when she saw the "final demand" notice that had been pushed under the door.

She sank to her knees and with a shaking hand she picked up

the envelop. "Please, please, let me find Jason... and soon." Only empty silence answered her.

B y the next morning, Lexie had her emotions under control. Before bed, she'd had a glass of wine—or two. Then she'd allowed herself the luxury of shedding a few tears, watched some funny animal videos on YouTube and gone to bed.

At five-thirty, she'd risen and gone for a short jog before getting ready for work. Unlike some people when they're upset, Lexie was an emotional eater. She'd scarfed down a big breakfast, filled her giant travel mug with coffee, and headed for Bad Boy Autos. No Starbucks for her.

Every spare dollar went into what she called her Freedom Fund. It was a separate bank account she'd asked Tom to set up in his name in case Jason learned of it. She was listed as an authorized user on the account, supposedly for business purposes, but the money was all hers. They were the only ones who knew about its existence.

Lexie would use the money to pay off the other bills Jason had stuck her with. She'd done the math, and with careful management and being frugal as hell, she could be out of debt in five years.

Because she had no large savings, and to stop the foreclosure on her cabin, she needed at least nine months of hefty mortgage payments besides the other debts he'd left her to pay. Alternatively, she needed to find Jason and retrieve the money he'd stolen. Suddenly, thirty days seemed short.

Pulling her Jeep into the parking lot, Lexie smiled when Zip Chang stepped outside his bay to see who had arrived. The young Chinese man smiled and waved. Lexie returned his greeting as she got out and grabbed her backpack, which she used instead of a purse.

"Hey, Lex. How goes it?" Zip asked as she drew closer.

"It goes just fine. How about with you?"

"Good. I brought donuts. They're in the break room," Zip informed her.

"You know I'll be all over them later on," Lexie said.

The other bane of her existence, Marcus, sat at his desk with a cellphone to his ear, drumming his fingers on his desk blotter. His gray eyes met hers, and the frown on his handsome face deepened. Lexie ignored him and continued on to the break room.

Tom stood by the coffeemaker, pouring some fragrant brew into a mug. A huge yawn gripped him as he turned to look at Lexie.

She smiled. "Baby keep you up again?"

Tom and his wife, Kendra, had become the proud parents of a baby girl, Matti, four months ago.

He stirred sugar into his coffee. "Yeah. She's living up to her name, 'lady of the house.' She started screaming at one this morning and woke Connor up. So, both of them were driving us crazy. Connor wanted to play, and Matti was fussy. We didn't get back to bed until almost four."

Lexie loved four-year-old Connor, who had adopted her as an aunt. She often babysat for him when Tom and Kendra went out.

"I'm sure Matti will settle into a routine soon," Lexie said. "I'll go get changed and get started. Don't want my pay docked for being late."

"Lex, I know you're pissed at me, but we can't afford to antagonize a man like Kade." Tom's eyes reflected his regret. "Journalists are notorious for using their platform when pissed."

Lexie gave a curt nod as she put up the defensive walls around her heart. "I know. Don't worry about it. I'll get it done and then I'll get him—and hopefully his brother—out of my life. No worries. I'll talk to you later."

She didn't wait for Tom to respond. A door at the back of the break room opened into a small locker room, complete with a shower and two changing stalls. Lexie grabbed her overalls from her locker and slipped them on over her jean shorts and turquoise tank top. She made sure her ponytail was secure and stuck her cellphone in her pocket.

Looking in the mirror over one of the two sinks, Lexie stared at her reflection and gave herself a pep talk. She had work to do, and she'd focus on the job, putting everything else out of her mind.

Only when the cellphone rang to say Kevin had found Jason would she breathe easy. Kevin and his team had tried to follow the money, but it looked as if Jason had it in cash, and that's why they had to find him soon. Not only could Jason sniff the money up his nose, someone could steal it. Nine months. He'd had the money for nine months. Hope of getting any of it back was slim, but she prayed there was enough to see if the bank would let her continue on a payment plan to pay the rest back… a proper mortgage. Only she'd have to explain what Jason had done. Would that get him in trouble? She thought the bank might not like the publicity of being conned.

The sick feeling churning in her stomach wouldn't go away. She may not have spent very much time at the cabin, but it represented the last fun time she'd spent with her mother, Clara, before the motor neuron disease ravaged her. It was also where, as Lexie sat holding her hand, Clara took her last breath.

She squeezed her eyes shut so the welling tears couldn't escape. She'd speak to Kade and tell him what she had learned. Kade might know where Jason would stay in Michigan, or who he'd stay with.

That decided, she straightened her spine and went to restore Kade's Alfa.

Chapter Three

A week later, Kade returned to Bad Boy Autos to check on the progress of his car. He'd told Tom that Lexie should do whatever felt right with the vehicle, giving her complete control. She was one of the most respected restorers in LA. She'd make his car purr.

Although he'd wanted to see Lexie sooner, he'd been away working on a story. Besides, knowing her as he did, he knew she'd have become defensive if he'd smothered her. As long as she was still hunting for Jason rather than letting the police do it, he could give her the space to work her magic, which would give her some time to adjust to him coming around more often.

At least he now had a plan of how to help her. The private detective he'd hired to find Jason had followed his trail to Michigan. When he found him, if Jason didn't have the money he'd stolen, he'd *give* Jason the money and watch him give it to Lexie to clear the debt. She'd never know it came from him.

Although a confident man, Kade didn't enjoy being a hard-ass or using intimidation tactics when dealing with people, but this time Jason had gone too far. He'd broken the law, and he prayed he could make his brother get the help he needed.

He wondered if he was doing his brother more harm by not

reporting his crime. On the one hand, prison might get him off the drugs, but on the other, it might simply feed his addiction. Kade knew drugs were rife inside.

It had always baffled him how a woman like Lexie could've fallen for Jason's shit.

They do say love is blind.

While Lexie was tough and didn't take shit from anyone, she was also kind and fun-loving with a soft center. Or she had been before Jason had gotten involved with drugs and started sleeping around on her. It had pained Kade to watch her suffer because of his brother. However, outside of trying to talk sense into Jason and offering to be a sounding board for Lexie, Kade hadn't gotten involved.

He wished to God he had. He should have run interference and pushed Jason into rehab. He'd held back because he had taboo feelings for his sister-in-law.

Despite his feelings for Lexie, he'd hoped for her sake that Jason would wise up and things worked out between them. Instead, Jason's behavior had only gotten worse. He'd crushed Lexie when he'd sold their restored 1960s Formula One race car. Then to mortgage her cabin and run off with the money and some track bimbo…

It had been the final blow, and Lexie had immediately started divorce proceedings.

Walking toward the garage, Kade saw Lexie's bay door was open and headed for it. A cacophony of revving motors and various air-compressed tools greeted his ears, filling Kade with excitement. Even though he'd never been a pro race car driver, he shared Jason's passion for fast cars and speed. He'd done his share of street and amateur racing, but he'd never considered that as a career.

Instead, he'd gone into journalism, writing about the racing circuit which led to a successful career, and also several *New York Times* bestselling suspense novels set around the professional racing circuit. He'd made millions, and now he lived a great life.

Money, women, vacation homes, helicopters, fast cars. He had it all.

Yet lately, something was missing. He was lonely. He wanted what Tom had, love with the right woman, and all the things that came with a family life, especially kids.

But most of the women he met only saw his celebrity and wealth. He wanted something deeper, real, and everlasting.

Why couldn't I have met Lexie first?

Approaching Lexie's bay, Kade saw his car up on the lift. Lexie stood underneath it with Sully, conferring with him about something to do with the rear axle.

Kade paused for a moment as he watched them. Lexie hadn't noticed him yet. Whatever Sully said had amused her, and her deep brown eyes shone as she laughed. The dimple in her right cheek appeared, and Kade had a sudden desire to kiss it—and every other inch of her. Even in her dirty navy-blue overalls, she was sexy as hell despite the fact they somewhat hid her delectable body.

It had always driven Kade crazy when she wore them— much more than the few times he'd seen her in a slinky dress or a bikini. Maybe it was because he knew what was under the overalls and he wanted to unwrap her like a candy bar.

Bringing his reaction to her under control, Kade entered the bay.

Lexie looked in his direction, and her smile faded when she recognized him. Kade tried to ignore his disappointment at the wary, irritated expression that settled on her beautiful features, but he wasn't quite successful.

"Hi." Kade gestured toward the car. "How's it going here?"

Based on Lexie's attitude the day he'd dropped off the Alfa, he thought talking about business first was the best course of action.

Sully said, "I'll leave you to it, Lex. Good to see you, Kade."

"Likewise," Kade replied.

He watched Sully walk away, a little jealous of the easy,

friendly rapport he and Lexie shared. Kade wanted that with her, and his determination to win her over intensified as he returned his attention to her.

L exie clenched her teeth when she saw Kade, then willed her jaw to relax. Watching him walk toward her in jeans with a white t-shirt that stretched tight across his well-muscled chest, a thread of female appreciation wrapped around her. He had a different build than Jason. Jason was shorter, about her height, 5'8"—that's how he'd fit in the racing cars. Kade was taller, about 6 feet, and all muscle.

It wasn't every man who could rock the shaved hair look, but Kade did it with ease. His short, almost black beard emphasized his strong jaw and drew attention to his sensual mouth. As her gaze roamed over him, Lexie noticed the tattooed armband around each bicep, amused by the fun names. The right one was labeled "thunder" while the left had been dubbed "lightning."

She couldn't hold back a smile as she asked, "You named your guns? That's pretty conceited."

Kade grinned and flexed his muscles, amused that she'd noticed. "Not conceited, just telling the truth. I'm the current boxing champ at my gym."

"I didn't know you boxed," Lexie said, trying to remember if Jason had ever mentioned it.

"There's a lot you don't know about me, Lexie."

The invitation in his voice made Lexie frown a little. He was trying to entice her into asking questions, but she resisted taking the bait.

"I guess so," she responded. "Well, I'll show you where we're at with things." She motioned for Kade to follow her and led him to the rear axle she and Sully had been discussing. "You really should've taken a better look at this car before you bought it. The car was stored somewhere with a lot of moisture exposure. Probably parked on grass and left uncovered. There's a lot of rust under here." She tapped the axle. "Including this. See this place here?"

Kade moved closer and looked at the rusted-out spot she'd indicated. "Yeah. That doesn't look good."

He stood so close that Lexie felt his body heat and smelled his citrus and spice cologne. The combination was delicious, and Lexie had to work hard to not lean closer and inhale it deep into her lungs.

Annoyed with herself, Lexie stepped away from him a little. "It's not. If I took this out on the road, I wouldn't get very far before it would snap. I'm surprised it didn't when it was loaded on the tow truck. It should be replaced."

"Damn," Kade muttered in dismay and turned his coffee-brown eyes on her. "Is the rest of it as bad as this?"

The car lover in Lexie sympathized with him. "Not all of it, but there's more wrong with it than there isn't. The floor in the front on the passenger side is rusted through, and three of the brake drums have to be replaced."

Kade passed a hand over his face and sighed. "Do you have an estimate yet?"

Lexie nodded. "Yeah. Look, Kade, this will cost a fortune. Are you sure you want to go through with it?"

Lexie bit her bottom lip as she waited for his answer. Although she didn't relish the idea of seeing Kade a lot, restoring the Alfa to its former glory excited her.

Watching his gaze travel over the underside of the car, Lexie knew Kade was a gorgeous guy. Those guns of his weren't the only thing impressive about him. Wide, chiseled chest, narrow, defined abdomen, tight ass, and powerful calves—all those attributes added up to one very tasty man.

A part of her had always been attracted to Kade, and she'd felt so guilty. Jason was his brother.

Did the fact that she found Kade attractive mean that she no longer loved Jason? Had it really been love at all?

If she'd loved Jason, she'd loved a Jason that never existed.

Disconcerted by her train of thought, Lexie shut them down and got back to business.

"Honey, with me, money's no problem. You know that. Let's do it."

Lexie's eyebrows lifted. "Okay. But you've got more money than sense." Lexie walked to the computer and woke it and logged into the invoicing system. Finding Kade's estimate, she printed it off and handed it to him. "Read it and weep."

Kade shot her a curious look and then studied the estimate. Lexie barely restrained her mirth as Kade's eyebrows climbed his forehead. She watched him scan the paper a second time before he pointed to a line of text.

"You have paint on here, but there's no cost and no description."

"Right. I was hoping you might let me give the little Alfa something more than a boring red paint job."

"You mean racing stripes or something?"

Kade's frown was adorable. She laughed. "No. But something tasteful to match the car. I came up with some ideas if you'd like to see them."

"Hell yeah."

Lexie kept a silly smile off her face and pulled a huge sketch pad from a shelf under the workbench top. Opening it, she started flipping pages, but after a couple, Kade stopped her.

"Damn, Lexie. I forgot what a kick-ass artist you are."

He tapped the detailed colored-pencil drawing of an old Ford pickup on the current page. On the drivers-side door, a depiction of a ranch, complete with a blue sky and sun overhead, graced the surface.

"Makes me want to buy a truck just so you can do that to it," Kade commented.

It was impossible for Lexie to ignore the pride his praise created. "That was for a job Sully had a little while ago. It was a 1960 Ford F-100. The customer wanted it restored as a birthday present for his dad, who was a rancher. He sent me a picture of their family's ranch and I created the design from it."

The way Kade's eyes lit up made Lexie smile. "Do you have any pics of the finished job?"

"Yeah. We take pics of all our jobs. Not only because we like to show them off, but as a proof of the work we do."

"Can I see them?"

Lexie shrugged. "Sure."

With a few more mouse clicks, she located the correct folder, pulled up the pics of the truck and moved out of the way.

Kade stepped in front of the computer and let out a low whistle. "That's incredible. I can't believe how much detail you got on it. There's even a horse and a cow."

Out of nowhere, sorrow hit Lexie, and she couldn't breathe for a moment while she fought it off. When the sharp pain in her heart faded to a dull ache, she said, "This was a really fun job because it was so different from most of the stuff I do. We don't have a lot of requests for country scenes on cars, so it was a nice change of pace." She swallowed hard. "It was almost a year ago. My first job when I started here, right after Jason stole our money and ran off with that whore. I owe Tom a lot for hiring me, even though Marcus didn't want him to."

Kade's mouth curved in a wry smile. "Let me guess; that's why you're putting up with me."

Guilt flickered across Lexie's face, but she had to be honest. "Yeah." Not caring to expound upon her reply, she changed the subject. "Anyway, let me show you the designs I came up with for your car."

She reached for the mouse, but Kade rested a hand on her forearm.

"I learned Jason's in Michigan. I have men there looking for him. I promise I'll find him in time."

"My P.I.'s there, too."

"Lexie, I'm not my brother. Please don't judge me by his actions. We're nothing alike. I'm not the bad guy."

Despite the sincerity in his eyes, Lexie couldn't let her guard down. Kade might not be his brother, but the Colter men still had a reputation where women were concerned. "You say that, but I remember you always had women lined up just itching to get into bed with you."

"I'm not married. I never disrespect the women I'm with." His expression grew shuttered. "Besides, just because they wanted me didn't mean I wanted them. Like I said, Lexie, there's a lot you don't know about me. Maybe it's time you learned what I'm really like."

Lexie's eyes widened. "What do you mean?"

Kade's friendly smile didn't put her at ease. "I mean, I'd like us to get to know each other a little better. I'm not your enemy."

Why this sudden need to know her? Was he trying to keep her on his side to save Jason? Pulling her arm away, Lexie wondered at the way her skin tingled from his touch. "I don't know what you want from me, Kade."

"I don't want anything from you. I just think it would be good for us to be on friendly terms while you work on my car. I'd rather have a good time instead of being at each other's throats, wouldn't you?"

Lexie resisted crossing her arms over her chest because she didn't want Kade to know how defensive she felt. "Do you know Jason mortgage my cabin?"

He looked at the ground. "Yeah. And I'm so thankful you haven't pressed charges."

"*Yet*. I haven't pressed charges yet."

He looked directly into her eyes. "Please give me a chance to make this right. If I can't find Jason, I swear I'll ensure you won't lose the cabin. If he goes to prison—"

"Stop. I would never want Jason to go to prison. He's sick. He has an addiction, and he needs help. Prison won't help him."

The relief on his face proved he loved his brother. "Thank you for being so understanding." He stood looking at her with a puzzled frown. "Very understanding. What are you not telling me?"

"My mother was an addict."

He waited for her to continue, but she wasn't up to sharing so, finally, he shrugged and added, "You understand then."

She forced her lips to curve into a small smile. "Yeah, I guess so."

Unlike hers, Kade's smile was genuine. "I sense there's a story there. One day, perhaps you'll share it."

Again, she said nothing.

He sighed. "Okay, so show me these designs."

Relieved that he'd changed the subject back to the matter at hand, Lexie flipped through her huge sketch pad until she found the first design. It was a picture of a beautiful Italian garden spread over the hood as if it was sprouting out of the engine and ready to climb the windscreen.

It took almost an hour for her and Kade to agree on the exact details, but he loved the garden idea. They tweaked it, and soon, it became a combination of both their ideas. It surprised her to learn that he had an artistic streak. His attempts at drawing were crude and often made her laugh, but his vision for his car was sound.

She'd gotten so caught up that Lexie was a little disappointed when they'd finished. Detailing cars and drawing were her passions, and it was nothing for her to spend hours talking about both.

As she closed her sketch pad and stowed it under the workbench, Kade asked, "So when do you think you'll finish it?"

"Well, giving you an exact time frame will be hard because finding original parts, or at least ones that are close, might take some time. I started looking for parts, but I didn't get too involved in case you didn't want to continue once you saw how expensive it would be," Lexie replied.

Kade pulled his keys out of a pocket. "I can understand that. Smart thinking." He turned, thoughtful as he looked at his car.

"But I *will* see this through until it's done. I don't care how long it takes. It may help take my mind off my brother."

"I hope we can find Jason before I finish this car, for his sake as much as mine."

He nodded. "Between your P.I. and my guys, I feel that it won't be long until we find where he is."

"All right. I'll keep you updated on how things are going," she said. "I guarantee that you'll be blown away, though."

"I'm counting on it," Kade said. "Well, I've taken up enough of your time. I'll see you soon."

"See ya." Lexie watched him walk through the bay door, out into the sunlight. Regret gnawed at her because she'd always assumed that Kade was a womanizer like Jason. Though, he was laying on the charm a bit too much. Surely, since he now understood that she'd never have Jason arrested, there was no need to flirt with her?

Perhaps he didn't believe her?

It didn't matter, though. He was just a client.

Looking up at the car on the lift, Lexie smiled as she walked over to it. She patted the tire the way people petted a dog. "All right, my diamond in the rough. Time to get started on making you shine."

Shoving Kade from her mind, Lexie was soon lost in her new labor of love.

Chapter Four

Thunder crashed overhead, and lightning flashes flickered outside the windows of the bay doors as Lexie installed brakes on Kade's car. She loved storms and relished the way the thunder reverberated through her body.

Finished with the front passenger side, Lexie moved over to the driver's side and started removing the old brake assembly.

Tom came over and looked at the car's undercarriage. "I'm glad you warned Kade that this will be an extensive job. Good thing Zip is a wiz with welding and metalworking. Fixing that rusted floor is gonna be a bitch."

"I know, but he loves fixing stuff like that," Lexie said. "He was a lucky find for you guys, and it was lucky for him you did."

Tom smiled as his gaze traveled to where Zip was putting new custom hubcaps on a Ferrari. "He's a good guy, and he needed the help."

Lexie's heart went out to Zip. "Yeah. Losing his parents and having to raise his brother hasn't been easy."

"No, it hasn't been, but he's doing a good job. Eddie's a real handful."

Lexie nudged Tom. "You should talk."

Grinning, Tom said, "You were just as bad as me, according to you."

Fond memories of all the hell she and her friends had raised as teenagers made Lexie chuckle. "True. Anyway, it will take a lot of work to get this thing in shape, but it'll be worth it in the end."

"I know that look."

"What look?"

"The one that says you're enjoying the hell out of a job. Does that mean you're not pissed at me anymore?"

Lexie's anger at Tom crumbled when he gave her a half-smile. "No, I'm not mad anymore. I'll be professional and do a great job."

Tom pulled her into a sideways hug. "I never doubted it. You know I'd never hurt you on purpose. I know this is hard, but maybe it'll be good for you, too."

Lexie's forehead creased as she looked up at him. "How do you figure? I'm trying to move forward, and every time Kade comes around, it just brings it all back. He's Jason's brother, Tommy."

Tom turned her to him and squeezed her arm. "I know, but you shouldn't hate the guy because he's Jason's brother. You're transferring your anger onto Kade, and that's really not fair. Maybe if you gave Kade a break, it would help you get past some of your bitterness."

Ignoring the stab of pain to her heart, Lexie said, "Look at you playing therapist. That's not really your style."

Tom laughed. "You can thank Kendra for that. Don't tell anyone, but she's sort of sanded down a few of my rough edges."

The love in Tom's eyes as he spoke of his wife twisted a shard of jealousy into Lexie's gut. She was thrilled that her friends had found happiness together, but it hurt to know she'd failed with Jason.

She forced a smile and patted Tom's chest. "Don't worry. Your secret's safe with me. Now, I'd better get back to work before my boss gets on my case."

Tom gave her arms a last squeeze and released her. "That's right. Quit slacking."

Lexie gave him a playful shove and resumed her work. As she did, she thought about what Tom had said and admitted he was right. Kade had always been nice to her.

Setting the ruined brake assembly to the side, Lexie knew that punishing Kade for Jason's transgressions was wrong.

Kade had shared the news about Jason being in Michigan with no prompting. She bit her lip. Trust had to be earned, and shit, she'd had her trust trampled by his brother. But she would reserve judgement and trust him for now.

Then she patted the worn tire hanging over her head. "Don't worry, sweetie. We'll get you shining and purring in no time."

———

Pulling up to Bad Boy Autos, Kade turned off the ignition and sat there for a few moments. All day his thoughts had been split between Lexie, his car, and the huge story he was working on. While he'd finished up a different article that morning, now Kade swung by to check on Lexie's progress with his car, and to talk to her bosses about the Erickson racing family.

They ran in the same circles, so they may have heard something about them that might be pertinent to his story.

Getting out, he pocketed his keys as he crossed the wet pavement. There was a break in the storms, but they expected the weather to turn nasty again later that afternoon. Sunshine peeked through sullen, gray clouds, turning the air muggy and making the asphalt steam as it heated under the sun's rays.

Kade entered the office, since all the bay doors were closed, and was greeted by Marcus, who came over to the counter that divided the lobby from the rest of the room.

"Hi, Kade."

"Marcus," Kade responded. "I came to see how Lexie's doing with the car."

"She's coming along with it. It's just taking a while to find all the right parts." He came around the counter. "I should thank you for giving us the job."

"I wanted to give Lexie something she'd love working on. I feel bad about the shitty way Jason treated her. She always supported Jason, and he wouldn't have been as successful without her. She didn't deserve what he did to her," Kade said.

"Your brother has a lot to answer for."

Kade nodded. "I know Jason's driving cost you your career. It cost Jason his, too. But I won't apologize for Jason, he has to do that himself."

Marcus' jaw tightened. "If anyone can find him before he ends up in the gutter dead."

Kade's temper flared, but he didn't comment on Marcus' insensitive remark. "Is it okay if I go talk to Lexie? At Marcus's nod, he left Marcus standing at the counter and walked through the open door to his right that led to the garage. Hard rock music blared, engines revved, and the sounds of many tools filled the huge space.

Along the way, he saw Tom and stopped to talk with him. "Hi. Sweet ride." He chin-nodded at the neon-blue Mustang.

"Yeah. Needs some fine-tuning."

"Do you have a few minutes to talk?"

Tom wiped his greasy hands on a rag. "Yeah, sure."

"You know the Erickson family, right?"

Tom nodded. "Yep. Why?"

"I'm doing an article on them and I'm looking for some insights from other racers."

"Okay. What do you want to know?"

Kade kept his tone conversational. "As a former competitor, what do you think of them?"

Growing pensive, Tom said, "A few people accused them of cheating, but I saw no proof of that. Marcus, neither. They could be pricks, but they're talented. They're also genius mechanics."

None of this was news to Kade, but he didn't let on. "What did people say they cheated at?"

"Illegal modifications to their cars, intimidation, that sort of stuff," Tom replied. "But none of the officials ever found anything whenever they checked out their cars."

"Intimidation? What kind?"

Tom closed the Mustang's hood. "Well, I wouldn't call it intimidation, really. More like screwing with other drivers' minds before a race. You know, shaking them up. Nothing will make you lose a race quicker than losing your temper. Charlie and Jack are real good at pissing people off."

"You ever buy any parts or anything through them?" His muscles tightened as he watched Tom closely.

There—he saw the flicker in his eyes.

"No."

"Why not?"

Tom shrugged. "I heard a few rumors. I like to know my parts haven't come off the back of a truck or that they're not made with inferior metal or are illegal copies."

"Are the rumors true?"

"Don't know and I don't care. I steer clear of Charlie and Jack Erickson, and you should, too. They're bad news."

Kade already knew that about the Ericksons' two drivers. "Yeah, they are. What are they like off the course?"

"Aren't you friends with them, Kade?"

"Yeah." He was. Until he'd seen something he shouldn't.

Tom grinned. "Then you know exactly what they're like. Hellions to the core, just like me and Marcus. Well, like I used to be, anyway."

Kade smiled. "Thanks for the info. Well, I'll go check on my car."

Tom chuckled. "You're sinking a lot of money into that wreck. Why are you doing it?"

"I have my reasons."

"Which means it's none of my business," Tom commented. "Okay. I'll see you later, man."

"Yeah. Later."

As he headed for Lexie's bay, Kade felt a spark of hope regarding his investigation of the Ericksons'.

The next moment, he spotted Lexie, and his pulse spiked at the sight of her leaning over the Alfa's engine from the side. Even in her overalls, her ass looked incredible, and a powerful urge to get his hands on it flowed through him. He curbed the impulse and forced his gaze elsewhere lest he be caught staring.

He walked over to stand at the front of the vehicle. "Hi, Lex."

She gazed up at him, and he thought she looked adorable with a small streak of grease on her cheek. He liked that she wasn't afraid to get her hands dirty.

She smiled, her eyes shining. "Hi, yourself. Came to check on your girl, huh?"

I wish you were my girl. Kade had to press his lips together for a moment to keep the words from tumbling out of his mouth. "Yeah. How is she?"

Lexie came out from under the hood and laid her socket wrench on the top of her tall tool chest on wheels. As she picked up a rag and wiped her hands, she let her gaze trail over Kade, and his body heated.

What's wrong with me? Knock it off. He wasn't here to get involved with Lexie. Not yet, anyway. They had to find Jason and put the past behind them before he could think about anything with Lexie.

"Well, she's a lot better than when you brought her in. All new brakes, air filter, and tires. I installed a new muffler system on her and put a new battery in it. Zip will work on fixing the floor this afternoon. He's a genius at welding and metal work," she informed Kade.

"Wow, you're really moving along with it."

"I did a ton of stuff on her, but I don't have time to rattle it all off. Do you want me to print off a work list up to this point?"

Kade nodded. "Okay, but only because I'm curious. Not because I'm checking on your work. I trust you completely, which is why I requested you for the job."

"Kade, about how I acted when you dropped the car off... I took my anger at Jason out on you, and that wasn't fair. I'm sorry."

Wow, he hadn't expected that. Hating the guilt in her eyes, Kade made a dismissive gesture. "Don't worry about it. I get it. I hate what he's done to you too."

She hung her head, but not before he saw tears welling. "Thanks. I appreciate that."

"You're welcome." He couldn't help asking, "How are you doing with everything?"

Lexie shrugged. "Better these days, I guess. But still no news. Have you heard anything more?"

"No. Trail's gone cold. He's not in Michigan. Or not anymore." Kade moved closer and noted the dark circles under her eyes. "When was the last time you had some fun?"

Surprised, Lexie didn't have an answer for him. "I...um..." She laughed. "Honestly? I really don't remember."

"That's what I thought. You need a distraction."

"A distraction? Like what?"

Kade took a deep breath and tried to keep his voice light. "How about dinner tonight?"

It was rare for Lexie to be struck speechless, but his invitation obviously shocked her. At length, she said, "Dinner?"

Kade couldn't help teasing her. "Yeah. You know, the meal you eat at the end of the day?"

Her arms wrapped round her waist. "I'm not sure that's a good idea, Kade."

He lowered his voice. "Just as friends, Lexie. Nothing more. We might talk strategy about where to go from here in regards to finding Jason. Time is marching on."

She nodded at that idea. Arching an eyebrow, she asked, "What kind of dinner?"

"Something that requires casual clothes. Jeans will work just fine."

"Nothing romantic, though?"

"Not even remotely romantic. I promise."

"Where would you take me?"

He held up an index finger and wagged it back and forth. "No, no. It's a surprise."

He watched all ranges of emotions flutter over her face, and his heart plummeted when he saw resignation.

"I appreciate the offer, but I just can't."

Kade sighed. "I figured you'd turn me down. Okay. Have it your way, but if you change your mind…"

Lexie nodded in response to the invitation he let linger between them. "Thanks."

"Sure. Now, how about that list?"

She hadn't wanted to say no. Guilt hit like a rampaging bull. Jason's image swam into his head, even though he tried to shut him out. *What a wanker, hitting on his girl when he's down and out.*

But then Jason didn't deserve Lexie after all he'd done to her.

He focused on the paper in his hand, and his eyebrows rose as he looked it over. "Holy shit. You already did all this? How much more does it need?" *Good thing I have a healthy savings account.*

Lexie laughed. "There's still about five things I need to fix before I can start the new paint job. I never start that until we finish everything else."

"Right. Well, I gotta go, but let me know how things are going."

"Okay. See you."

He walked away, willing himself not to look over his shoulder. Perhaps her saying no was for the best. He didn't want to piss her off and have her take it out on Jason.

Chapter Five

"So, I hear Kade asked you out."

Lexie looked up from studying the drawing she'd been working on and almost choked on the sip she'd just taken.

Sully smiled and sat down across from her at a table in the break room. "I think you should go."

Lexie slapped her pencil down on her sketch pad and folded her arms over her chest. "I will kill that little nark. Apparently, Zip can't keep his lips zipped."

Sully's grin irritated Lexie even more. "Actually, it wasn't Zip —this time. I overheard it myself. It wasn't like Kade was being secretive about it. Anyone walking by would've heard it, which a few of us were."

Lexie rolled her eyes and groaned. "Does the whole garage know?"

"Yep."

"Oh, joy. Color me thrilled." Sarcasm laced Lexie's statement.

"We also know you turned him down."

Lexie fixed him with a glare. "You know what amazes me? That a group of supposedly big, tough he-men are just as interested in gossip and meddling in people's business as women.

This is why I'm not friends with many women. I hate drama. Looks like I'm working in the wrong place to avoid that. Doesn't seem like there's much testosterone around here."

Sully barely raised an eyebrow over her insult. "Why d'you turn him down? You need to have some fun."

"I have plenty of fun," Lexie said, knowing she was going to hell for lying. "Besides, I'm going out with Pace for dinner on Thursday night." She was. And for once, she was looking forward to some male company.

Sully let out a short bark of laughter. "Really? That's great."

Lexie swore. "Now *that* will be all around the mechanic's bay too."

Sully winked at her. "No, it won't. Cross my heart... Did Kade have any further news on Jason's whereabouts?"

"He's not in Michigan." She shook her head. "I just want this over with. I feel like my life is on hold. A divorce is painful, but it's also closure."

"Yeah, I get it," Sully replied. "After my divorce, I just wanted to move on and forget all the crap that happened. Thing is, unless you have the mentality of a frozen shark, you can't do that. I tried, but it doesn't work. I learned that to get through terrible times, you must deal with the pain until it doesn't hurt as much."

Lexie folded her arms over her stomach. "I've been hurting for so long, Sully. I just want to find Jason, get my finances sorted, and get on with my life. Kade is simply a means to an end. Both of us want the same thing—to find Jason. If not for Jason, we'd have nothing in common."

"You could be right. But he can find Jason without you, you can finish his car without his help, so why is he hanging around?"

Lexie chewed her bottom lip and realized she'd been thinking the same thing. "I think he's worried I'll report Jason to the police."

"Police? What for?"

Sully was all fatherly concern, and she loved him for it. "Don't worry. It's just he… Never mind."

"I'm beginning to hate this guy."

She hugged Sully. "Don't. You of all people know what addiction can do to a person."

"You really know how to bring a guy down to earth," Sully responded. "But, yeah. Doesn't mean I have to be a fan of Jason's."

Lexie said, "I'm not exactly a fan either, but I'm still his wife until he signs those bloody papers, and I want to help him if I can."

Rising, Sully sighed. "Someone needs to, but remember, you can't help him if he doesn't want help. Don't waste your life on a lost cause. Be there if he needs you, but move on if he doesn't."

Lexie's mind whirled as Sully left the break room. She hadn't thought past getting the money back from Jason. What would she do when she found him? Did she have it in her to help Jason again, like Nick, her mother's last boyfriend, had helped her mother? She'd tried so hard, but Jason had kicked her around like an old football you took out of the closet now and then to play with.

She returned her attention to her drawing, but a small voice inside kept whispering it was time to let Jason go. No matter what happened, she was done. Let Kade look out for his brother.

She resumed working and had just started to get lost in it when her phone rang. Pulling it out of her pocket, she looked at the number on the caller ID, but didn't recognize it.

She hit the answer button. "Hello?"

"Lexie?"

Lexie pulled in a startled breath. "Jason?"

"Yeah. Look, I'm sorry about the car, but it was mine, you know? I mean, it was in my name, so I had the right to sell it."

Lexie knew that flying off the handle was useless, so she swallowed her rage and her need to say, "but not my cabin—you had no right to mortgage the cabin."

43

"Jason, where are you? Are you in LA?"

"No. Chicago."

Shit! "When are you coming to LA? We need to sign the divorce papers."

"Divorce papers? Don't leave me now—"

"Me leave you? Get real. You left me months ago." Lexie's grip tightened on her cellphone and she had to force herself to loosen it, so she didn't crush it. "Our marriage is over."

"I said I was sorry. It was the drugs."

She tried to find her Zen. "You have a problem, Jason. You need to get help before it kills you."

"I'm trying." Jason's voice had taken on the tone that had once melted her heart, but it left her glacier-cold now.

"Kade's worried about you, too. He's desperate for you to come home to LA."

"Kade? Have you been seeing Kade?" Anger filled his tone. "You keep away from my brother!" And with that, he hung up.

Damn. She dialed Kevin. "I just got a phone call. He says he's in Chicago."

"I'll see if I can trace the call. I have a few friends in the force who owe me. I'll be in touch."

Looking at the art supplies strewn over the table, Lexie knew the call had broken her concentration too much to do any more quality work that night. With a groan of frustration, she put her art stuff in her big backpack and slung it over her shoulder. As she walked through the office, she saw Marcus at the computer on the service counter.

He flicked a glance her way. "Night, Lex."

"Night, Marcus."

Perhaps Marcus was warming to her. He'd actually said goodnight to her.

Pulling onto South Figueroa Street, Lexie gave a sigh of relaxation as she picked up speed and then turned onto CA-110, heading for Echo Park. Driving was another way she coped with stress. She'd put a lot of miles on the Jeep over the past few months, just cruising around LA on nights she couldn't sleep. Tonight, she'd stop at her favorite bar and listen to some music.

Ten minutes later, Lexie found a parking spot and got out. Even though she could barely hear the throbbing pulse of base, she knew the music would be almost deafening inside. Joe Brady, the owner, had virtually soundproofed the place to cut down on the cops harassing him about noise violations.

Opening the door, she encountered the bouncer assigned to card people as they came in. Lexie knew Tony, and they exchanged hellos before she entered the main bar area. A long, chrome-gilded bar stretched out before her, in the middle of which eight racing car tires were affixed in a row. Fifteen chrome-plated stools were upholstered in red leather. All the metal gleamed in the bright lighting from the numerous head-lights situated all around the room.

Diedre Knight, one of the bartenders, waved to Lexie from behind the bar. Lexie smiled and headed over, taking one of the last three empty stools. "Hey, Diedre."

Diedre's blue eyes shone with humor as she motioned toward the crowded barroom. "It's a big crowd tonight, so busy. What can I get you?"

"It's been one of those days, so a beer is in order. Whatever's on tap is okay."

"All right."

While she waited for her beer, Lexie glanced around the bar, nodding to some people she knew and noticing a few men glancing her way. Even though she wasn't interested, she enjoyed knowing she was still attractive to the opposite sex. Diedre sat her beer in front of her. Lexie thanked her and took a sip.

"Didn't think I'd see you here tonight."

Any semblance of a smile fled from Lexie's expression as she turned to meet Marcus' eyes. "I'm allowed out now, I'm over twenty-one."

He downed a shot. "I didn't know you were coming here. You know, that's no way to talk to your boss."

"I don't see my boss. He's at home with his wife and kids."

A tiny thrill of satisfaction ran through Lexie at Marcus' scowl.

"Lexie, the only reason you still have a job is because Tom and I have an agreement." His silver-gray eyes cooled a couple of shades. "He let you in the door because you're friends, but the only thing keeping you employed is the quality of your work. But if that starts to go downhill…"

Marcus' meaning was clear to Lexie. Her cheeks burned with indignation, but she restrained the emotion. Keeping her job was more important than antagonizing him. Suddenly, she heard her grandmother's voice in her head. *You catch more flies with honey, dear.* She'd spent her summers at her grandmother's farm in Idaho, and Charlotte Emery had been full of sage, old-fashioned advice. Lexie applied that particular adage to the current situation.

She swallowed a little pride as she raised her chin a fraction. "Marcus, I owe you an apology."

The way his dark eyebrows shot up almost made Lexie laugh. "For what?"

Lexie took a moment to gather her thoughts, so she didn't sound like an idiot. She hadn't been planning on having this conversation with Marcus tonight, but something nudged her to continue. "I shouldn't have acted like a bitch to you in the past, but I'd like to explain why I did."

A suspicious frown settled on Marcus' face. "Is this a joke?"

Lexie shook her head. "No, I promise. You know what Jason is like and everything he's been putting me through, right? I know what he put you through and I can see why you'd want to blame me too. We all know he shouldn't have been racing that day, and even though clipping your car was an accident, if he was drugged up… It was his fault. Not mine. I've never touched drugs. You're tarring me with the same brush, just like I was with Kade. I thought you were happy owning Bad Boy Autos, but I see the resentment in your eyes every time you look at me. You really want to be driving on the circuit, don't you? I must be a constant reminder of all you've lost."

"I try not to think about Jason Colter, but…"

Meeting his gaze, Lexie replied, "You're a lot like Jason— reckless, wild, irresponsible, and you sleep with anything in tight jeans or a miniskirt." Lexie held up a hand when he would've responded. "Just don't end up like the man you despise. Don't drink yourself into alcoholism. Don't let Jason beat you."

Marcus leaned back in his chair as a surprised laugh escaped him. "Wow. Genuine concern for me."

Lexie grinned, enjoying catching him off-guard. "Honestly, I'm kind of surprising myself."

He arched an eyebrow as he looked down at the drink he held in his hand. "I guess you're making sense." He looked at her as his smile faded. "I don't want Jason to win anything. And I'll never end up like him."

"Probably not, because you have a family that loves you. They won't let you self-destruct. Just watch the booze."

Marcus' jaw tightened. "Don't start. I get enough of that from Kendra. She keeps saying I should grow up. We *were* pretty wild in racing circuit days, weren't we?"

"I know, and that's what stuck in my mind all this time instead of seeing that you've changed," Lexie said. "I mean, you've settled down some, opened a successful business, and become more involved with your family."

He let out a derisive snort. "That only happened because I got hurt. Because of Jason. If I hadn't, I'd still be out on the racing circuit, doing what I love the most."

"True, but you turned what happened around and made something positive out of it. Unlike Jason, who dealt with it by turning to drugs."

Marcus shifted on his stool, the movement conveying his

discomfort in talking about the situation. "Okay, I think this Hallmark moment is over."

Lexie cracked up, which drew a laugh from Marcus. Sobering, she said, "Look, the bottom line is that constantly fighting isn't good for us, and it's not good for business." She stuck a hand out to Marcus. "Truce?"

His measuring stare made Lexie a little afraid that she'd overstepped, but after a few moments, Marcus shook her hand. "Truce—so long as you're not coming onto me."

Another woman would've been offended, but Lexie found Marcus' leery attitude hysterical. "I'm not. Trust me," she assured him in a humor-laced voice.

He smiled and released her hand. "Good. And on that note, I'm going to the head. See you in the morning."

"Okay." Lexie watched Marcus saunter away from the bar. She didn't have any delusions that she and Marcus would ever be bosom buddies, but she hoped that they wouldn't fight as much. And she hoped his drinking never became a problem.

When she finished her beer, she ordered a double bourbon to nurse while the band played, and then headed for a small table along the far wall that had just been vacated. From that vantage point, she could see the stage where the band was doing a sound check. Renegade Blues was a great cover band, but they also played some original songs. Lexie sipped her drink and looked forward to their performance.

She jumped when someone said her name and tapped her shoulder. A jolt of surprise ran through her as Kade moved to the other side of the table.

"Hi. Fancy meeting you here." His smile made his eyes gleam.

"Oh. Hi."

Kade indicated the empty chair across from her. "Mind if I join you?"

Lexie sighed inwardly. She didn't want him to, but she

couldn't find a polite way to refuse. "Um, sure. That would be nice."

Kade chuckled as he dragged the chair over to her side. "You're lying, but I appreciate the hospitality."

Lexie had thought she'd pulled off the fib, but Kade had seen right through her. Of course, he was a journalist and had great powers of perception.

An unexpected prickle of awareness spread through her as Kade sat down. She was further disconcerted when her nipples tightened in response to his nearness. *I really need to have sex.*

"Are you here to see the band?" she asked, glad that she was wearing a padded bra that hid her reaction.

Kade leaned forward and rested his forearms on the table. He wore an old pair of black jeans and a black leather vest over a red t-shirt. He looked relaxed, casual, and hot, she admitted to herself. She liked the minty scent of his aftershave and the way he'd trimmed his beard. It made him look manly and tough. His edgy style made him resemble a race car driver or a pit crew member instead of a well-known writer.

Motioning toward the stage, he replied, "Troy Devlin, the drummer, is a friend of mine, and he bitched me out because I hadn't come to see the band play in a while."

Lexie said, "I didn't know you knew anyone in the band. They're great."

"Yeah, they are. So, who are you here with?"

It annoyed Lexie when she suddenly felt embarrassed that she was stag, but she wasn't going to let Kade see that it bothered her. "I needed some alone time, so I just came to listen to the band and veg out a little."

Kade grinned as he leaned closer. "And here I am ruining that plan—which I think sucks, by the way."

"It does, huh?" Lexie took a sip of her drink and straightened in her chair to put a little distance between them. "Do you have a better idea?"

"Yeah. You need to have some fun. I don't think you've had enough lately."

Fun wasn't her top priority, and she wished that he hadn't shown up. She was trying to chill and forget her troubles for a while, and Kade just brought it all back.

"Look, don't tell me what I need or don't need," she said. "I'm a big girl and I can take care of myself." She pushed her unfinished drink away and stood up. "Have a good night, Kade. I'll call you when I've made more progress on your car."

Frustration burned through Kade as he watched Lexie rise. He hadn't meant to offend her with his teasing, and he couldn't let her leave without clearing the air. He took her wrist in a light grasp. "Wait a sec, Lexie. I'm sorry. I was just kidding. I wasn't trying to tell you what to do. Honest."

Her stormy eyes met his for several long moments before her posture relaxed. "I believe you. I'm the one who's sorry. Jason used to tell me how I should feel, or that I was wrong to feel a certain way."

Kade rose to his feet. "I wasn't doing that."

Her pretty lips curved into a wry smile, and Kade resisted the strong urge to kiss her. "I know. I have to quit judging people based on his actions. It's not fair."

Kade realized that he was still holding her wrist and let it go. "I understand, but I would never insult your intelligence that way. You're a mature woman and you know your own mind."

"Thanks. I appreciate that."

"No problem. How about a game of pool before you leave? The band should be on soon. Stay for one song, at least. I can even introduce you to my friend."

He wished he could take those words back as they came flowing out. He didn't want his friend catching sight of Lexie. And that thought scared him silly.

A smug look settled on her face. "Are you sure you want to play against me? I'm sort of a pool shark."

He nodded. "That's why I asked you. I like a challenge."

"All right. Ten bucks says I beat you."

Her assertion brought a grin to Kade's face. "You're on. After you," he said, making a sweeping gesture toward the pool tables.

He was sure the sly look she sent him wasn't meant to be flirtatious, but it touched off his desire for her nonetheless. Try as he might, he couldn't keep his gaze from straying to her shapely ass as he followed her.

A pool table opened up as they neared, and Kade quickly claimed it. He put quarters in and the balls rolled into the open slot. "Do you want to rack them?" he asked Lexie.

"No, you go ahead."

Once Kade was finished, he rolled the white cue ball to the head of the table. "You break."

While he'd been racking the balls, Lexie had chosen a pool stick from the ones lining the wall and rubbed chalk over the tip. "Sure."

Kade lifted the rack and stepped back. Lexie situated the cue ball on the head spot and leaned over. Kade's body heated when the movement stretched her tank top across her breasts, revealing a tantalizing glimpse of cleavage. To distract himself, he went to pick out his own stick and reined in his libido.

Lexie shot the cue ball down the table. It hit the 1-ball dead-on with a loud crack and the other balls scattered. The striped 10-ball zoomed into a corner pocket, and Lexie flashed Kade a cocky grin. "I got stripes."

"Lucky break," he responded.

"Nothing lucky about it."

"We'll see."

When Lexie made two more shots in quick succession, Kade knew he was in for a battle. She sank another ball before scratching.

Kade laughed at her flub, but she just shrugged and said, "I thought you'd like a turn."

"Sure you did. You might as well sit down now that it's my turn."

"Nah. I don't think I'll be waiting very long."

Jibes and a lot of laughter accompanied the rest of the game. When Lexie had two balls left, both of which sat near a side pocket, she re-chalked her cue.

Kade watched as she paced around the table, considering her next shot. She moved gracefully, her hips swaying a little with each step. While she concentrated, she chewed on her bottom lip, which got Kade thinking about kissing her again.

Finally, she said, "Eleven-ball, corner pocket, and the nine-ball in the side pocket," pointing at each of the corresponding pockets.

"Getting tricky now, hmm?" Kade commented.

"I warned you," she said in a singsong voice.

"Yeah, yeah. Just take your shot."

Strains of electric guitar permeated the air as Lexie took careful aim. She thrust her stick forward and the cue ball streaked across the table. It hit the two striped balls, which fired off in opposite directions, each hitting their intended pockets.

Lexie let out a triumphant whoop while Kade groaned in dismay. "Shit! I can't believe you made that shot."

"Believe it, babe, 'cause it just happened!"

Kade laughed at her retort, glad that she was having fun. "Yeah, well, it ain't over yet. Still have to sink that eight-ball, *babe*."

In response, Lexie pointed at the far corner pocket with her cue. "Eight-ball, corner pocket."

Seconds later, Kade shook his head when the black ball dropped into the pocket.

Lexie came around the table and held out her hand, palm up. "Pay up, Kade. Time for me to collect my money and be on my way."

Kade was having a great time, and he didn't want Lexie to leave yet. "Not so fast. Let's go again."

Lexie's confident smile flashed as she shrugged a shoulder. "Okay. You must like losing money. If I agree to another game, what are we playing for?"

"Let's up the stakes," he replied, stepping a little closer. "If you win, I'll pay you thirty bucks, but if I win, you have dinner with me."

Lexie's breath caught, and she choked a little, making her voice sound froggy. "Have dinner with you?"

"Yeah."

Lexie planted her hands on her hips in annoyance. "We talked about this, Kade."

"Lexie, why are you so afraid of a friendly dinner?"

Like a cat, her name being said in the same sentence as the word "afraid" made her hackles rise. If she could, she'd spit and scratch his face.

"I'm not afraid, Kade, I just don't need any complications at work, or any more in my life, period."

"I don't want to complicate your life. I'd just like to show you a nice time. That's all. But if you don't have the stones to take a gamble and play me…" His unspoken challenge hung in the air between them.

He'd caught her in a trap. She was all about saving face.

"All right. You're on."

He didn't care about hiding his grin. He was having fun. "Awesome. Let's get to it."

Lexie chuckled and racked the balls. Kade broke, and the game was on. The stakes were even higher now, and Lexie approached each shot with painstaking caution. Kade wasn't taking any prisoners and sank three of his balls in a row, leaving only the 8-ball.

"So, Lex, what night is good for you?" he asked as he prepared to take his next shot.

"Cocky, aren't ya. It's not over yet. Are you ready to lose thirty bucks?" she countered.

Kade smiled and took aim.

To his surprise Lexie folded her arms under her breasts, pushing them up and giving him a great view down her bra. She was playing dirty.

He inwardly laughed as he took his shot after taking in the show. She barely kept from dropping her head as defeat smacked her in the face. He wouldn't gloat; that would see her spitting tacks.

Taking a breath, she put a resigned smile on her face. "Guess I better dust off my nice clothes. Congrats, Kade."

"You sound like having dinner with me is the kiss of death."

"I'm just wondering at the motive. Why are you so desperate to wine and dine me? I've told you Jason's safe from a jail cell—well, from *me* anyway."

Kade gritted his teeth. He wondered at his own motives, too. "I really don't know. How's that for honesty?"

Lexie's mouth dropped open. She closed it and asked, "Where are you taking me?"

"That's a surprise. What time is good for you?" What the hell was he doing? And why? Why did this woman stir him so?

"Okay. Pick me up at the shop around six," she said. "I get off at five and I can be ready by then."

He wanted to high-five someone, but he just said, "Six it is, then."

On a smile that said she knew he was full of crap, she added, "Say hi to your friend in the band for me. I'll catch him next time. I'm heading out. See you."

Kade said, "Ok. Good night."

He watched her weave her way through the crowded bar, and his groin tightened. He should feel the guilt start about now, but it didn't.

Just then, his phone rang. When he saw the number, he merely said, "What's the news?"

"It's hard to follow a money trail when Jason's got so much cash. But he is in Chicago. Just not in his usual haunts. No one's seen him, except a cab driver that picked him up from the airport. He dropped him at a motel near the waterfront, but he left the next day."

"Damn. Keep looking."

"The team is working overtime, but it's as if he's become a ghost. With no credit card purchases, we're flying blind. Maybe we should come back to LA and regroup."

"No. He's in Chicago. Just find him."

"Okay. It's your money." And the phone went dead.

Suddenly the euphoria over a date with Lexie died. What the fuck was he doing with his brother's wife? The divorce wasn't even through, and Jason was fighting his demons on his own.

Jason had once looked up to him. Hero worshipped, in fact. Then he'd had success on the racing circuit, and the fame, money and women went to his little brother's head. Overnight, Jason become a man Kade didn't recognize—or like.

If only he'd taken more interest in Jason's life. But when Jason brought Lexie to visit for the first time before they'd married, he'd had to pull back. The sudden protectiveness and possessiveness she stirred deep inside made warning bells peal.

He should have stuck around. Perhaps he could have stopped Jason's slide into drug addiction.

He downed a rum and Coke and shook his head. If Lexie couldn't stop him, then why did Kade think he could?

His mother was right. Jason was weak.

As he made his way out to the waiting Uber, he wished he could hold his brother and tell him everything would be okay.

He had to find him before it was too late.

Chapter Six

Lexie looked at herself in the locker-room mirror at work and debated about wearing lip gloss. She wanted to look nice, but not too nice, lest she give Kade the wrong idea. This *wasn't* a date. No, this was just dinner with a... What did she call Kade? She didn't like the idea of continually calling him her brother-in-law—soon to be ex-brother-in-law, she hoped—but could she consider him a friend? She supposed so.

Lexie decided on deep rose lipstick instead of the lip gloss and rummaged around in a small compartment in her backpack for it. It would look pretty, but not sexy. She applied it and a little mascara and looked at herself again. Her dark blue jeans and powder-blue buttoned-down shirt weren't fancy, but she felt sexy anyway.

Sexy. Why did she want to feel sexy?

"That'll do," she mumbled to herself and put her things away.

As Lexie slung her bag over her shoulder and headed out front to wait for Kade, she hoped he wasn't late. She'd already endured some ribbing from Tom about their outing, and she didn't want to hear any more. Entering the office, Lexie was relieved to find it empty, indicating that Tom and Marcus had already left for the day.

The clanking sounds of tools and the steady drumbeat of music meant that at least one mechanic was still working. She avoided the shop and went to stand outside the office door. It was a mild evening, with little humidity and no sign of rain. Lexie wished she was heading home instead of going with Kade. It would be a nice night to sit out on her miniscule patio and sip some wine while she watched the sun go down.

It wasn't long before Kade drove into the parking lot in his sleek, look-at-me silver Mercedes GT and stopped in front of her. He surprised her by getting out and coming around to the passenger side.

"Hi, Lexie. You look nice," he said, opening the door.

Lexie blinked a few times. She couldn't remember if Jason had ever opened a door for her. Realizing she was staring at Kade, she gave herself a mental shake and smiled. "Hi. Thanks. So do you."

She meant it. His jeans rode low on his trim hips and his short-sleeved blue t-shirt showcased his muscular chest and arms.

His smile made her pulse rise a little. "Thanks. Ready?"

"Yeah."

Kade held the door while she got in and shut it for her. His gentlemanly behavior, which seemed at odds with his tough-guy appearance, flattered her. He slid into the driver's seat and the fine hairs on Lexie's arms stood up over his sudden nearness. The car interior seemed to shrink until Kade filled her vision.

He shut his door and the sound jarred her out of the sudden spell he'd unknowingly cast over her. To hide her confusion, Lexie reached for the seat belt and buckled it. When she looked up, her gaze collided with Kade's, and he smiled.

"All set?"

"All set," she confirmed.

He put the car in gear and pulled out of the parking lot.

Lexie couldn't help admiring the calm, confident way Kade drove as they headed toward the downtown area of LA. He remained cool even when someone cut him off or tailgated him. Jason had a horrible case of road rage. As a racing driver, Jason thought he owned the road. Riding with him had always set Lexie's teeth on edge, and his almost constant yelling often gave her a headache. It was a relief to drive with someone like Kade.

As they traveled down the streets, the quality of the neighborhoods deteriorated, which made Lexie a little nervous.

"Where are we going?" she asked. "I don't know of any nice restaurants down here."

"Me neither. We're not going to a restaurant."

Lexie watched men on the street with a little trepidation. They'd started arguing, and there was a lot of emphatic gesturing going on. "Then where are you taking me? A food truck or something?"

"No. I'm taking you for the best spaghetti dinner you'll ever have," Kade said.

Looking around at the dilapidated, graffiti-riddled buildings, Lexie couldn't figure out where Kade meant. Some sections of the downtown area had seen rebirth since the early 2000s, but there were still areas, especially close to Skid Row, that had improved little. The neighborhood they were driving through didn't hold much promise.

Soon, Kade slowed down and took a right turn into a parking lot next to a long, squat building. Many of its dingy-brown bricks were cracked, and it needed repainting. Looking it over, Lexie noticed that while the building was rundown, the windows were clean, as was the parking lot. There was no litter, and while the thin strips of grass outlining the far edges of the lot were brown and dried up, they were neatly trimmed. Someone took pride in the place's appearance.

Kade pulled into a spot between a big, mint-green Chevy truck and a silver Lincoln Town Car and killed the engine.

"Are you going to tell me where we are now, man of mystery?" Lexie asked.

Kade laughed. "We're at the Little Street Underground Mission."

Lexie shook her head. "The what?"

"You heard me."

"You brought me to a mission for a spaghetti dinner? I've heard of being a cheapskate, but this takes the cake." Lexie laughed.

"No, Lexie. We're not here to eat. Well, not until a little later on," Kade said. "I volunteer here a few times a month serving meals. I'm on the schedule tonight."

Lexie looked at the ugly building and then back at Kade. "No wonder you said don't dress fancy."

Kade's smile didn't dim as he took the keys out of his ignition. "I promise you that in two hours, you'll be sitting down to some fine Italian dining."

When he got out of the car, Lexie just sat there for a moment.

"C'mon, Lex! There are hungry people in here who need us to serve them."

Lexie glanced at the building again, and then turned her gaze back to Kade's expectant expression. How amazing for a man who has it all, to want to help those who have nothing. Definitely different to his brother. Jason considered no one but himself. Like a block of ice cracking in the sun, her heart warmed. This was the type of man a woman would be proud to have at her side, to share her life with. Whoa, where did that thought come from? But she couldn't help love that he wanted to share this with her. He really seemed to be trying to prove he was not his brother—nothing like him, in fact.

She'd already told him she would press charges, so perhaps he really did just simply want to impress her. Get to know her. He'd guessed money didn't impress her, but this softer, kinder side to such an alfa male was intoxicating. She felt her face flush with heat. Kade could have almost any woman he wanted. Did he really want her?

She looked into his handsome face and decided perhaps she'd see where this lead—but cautiously.

"You certainly know how to impress a lady. I love this idea. You are full of surprises."

"I hope that's a good thing?"

Lexie said, "I guess we'll have to see. Let's go."

She started for the sidewalk in front of the building, but Kade caught her arm. "The kitchen entrance is this way. It's quicker."

His warm hand on her skin made Lexie's heartbeat leap. "Okay. Lead on."

Kade released her and strode toward the back of the building. They reached an ugly brown door, and Kade shot her a grin as he turned the handle. "Prepare for bedlam."

"I'm sure I can handle it," Lexie said.

Kade opened the door and motioned her inside.

For the first time today, Lexie looked forward to tonight—the man by her side too big a part of that happiness for her peace of mind.

Chapter Seven

It was almost ten p.m. when Kade dropped Lexie off at Bad Boy Autos to pick up her car. He drove up to the office and cut the engine.

"Admit it. You had a good time tonight."

Kade watched her closely, and Lexie couldn't hold back a smile at his smug statement. "It was interesting, to say the least."

Kade shifted in his seat to face her a little more. "C'mon, be honest. You liked it."

Lexie crossed her arms over her stomach and nodded her head. "Okay, yes, I had a good time. I didn't realize ministers could be so funny. Pastor Sal is hysterical, and I love the way he and Elouise razz each other."

"Yeah, Elouise keeps her hubby in line," Kade said. "They liked you, too, especially Elouise. She thought we were a thing until I explained the situation."

Lexie said, "She said the same thing to me, but I set her straight right away."

"Good. We don't need any misunderstandings. I told anyone who asked that we were just friends," Kade assured her. *Easy does it.* He didn't want to look too closely at why he didn't say "she's my sister-in-law."

Lexie looked out the windshield at the darkened garage as she pondered his words. "Friends. Are we, Kade?"

"Would that be so terrible?" He wished he knew what she was thinking.

"I've just never thought of you as more than Jason's brother." Something flickered in her dark eyes, but Lexie didn't elaborate.

His left shoulder lifted in a nonchalant shrug. "I know, but that doesn't mean we can't get to know each other a little better while you're working on my car."

Toying with a zipper on her bag, Lexie said what Kade had been expecting for days. "You never wanted to know me better when I was married to Jason. I thought you blamed me for his behavior."

Caught. What could he say to that? He opened his car door and got out. She smiled as she realized that he was coming around to open her door.

When he did, she alighted, but he blocked her path.

"Lexie, I don't think you believe men and women can be just friends."

Her mouth dropped open in shock, and she couldn't respond for a moment. "What? Why would you think that?"

"You seem to think we can't be friends, so maybe your only friends with other women."

"That's bullshit," she shot back. "Most of my friends are guys, and you know it. Tom is my best friend, and Sully is like an older brother to me, and—"

"So, why am I different?"

Lexie took a step back. "Hold on, isn't that what I just asked you? Why do you want to be," her fingers made quote marks in the air, "friends."

"Touché."

They stood staring at each other; the silence sending his nerves screaming. One of his hands held the car door open and the other one rested on the roof, trapping Lexie. Her fragrance stirred every cell in his body.

"Kade, I think you're a good guy, but I—"

"Don't want any complications. So you've said."

What had he expected? She was getting a divorce from his brother, for God's sake. She'd probably never thought of him in the way he thought of her... or wanted her.

"That's right. Look, I did have a really good time tonight, and you were right about the food being fantastic. Who knew a food-kitchen staff could cook like that?"

Kade smiled and stepped away from the car, his guilt flaring as usual when he was around her. "Well, it helps when the people running it are former chefs. There's nothing they can't make. They like feeding the less fortunate the same meals they made in their restaurant—albeit on a budget."

Lexie took her keys from her bag and slung it over her shoulder. "You said they saved you. What did you mean?"

He thumped her shoulder. "That's a story for another time, pal."

Lexie laughed. "Pal?"

Kade flashed a grin at her before walking around the car. "Yeah. Pal. More than an acquaintance, but not quite a friend. Night, Lex."

Lexie seemed amused by his evasiveness. "Don't I even get a hint?"

K ade came back around the car. Something happened as he walked toward Lexie. His strides held athletic grace, and she remembered him saying that he boxed. The image of him half-naked and sweaty made her mouth go dry. He suddenly seemed to move in slow-motion, like the hot hero in an action-movie scene.

Her gaze traveled over him, and she couldn't help comparing him to his brother. He wasn't flashy like Jason. He didn't have that movie star quality, but there was an unmistakably masculine aura about Kade that made women want to fall into bed with him. A quiet strength and dignity about the man.

She used to thread her fingers through Jason's thick shoulder-length hair, but she suddenly wondered what it would feel like to run them over Kade's prickly scalp.

Kade's dark eyes gleamed with amusement as he closed in on Lexie. There was also a warmth to his gaze that she couldn't recall ever seeing in Jason's. A smile curved his mouth in a sexy half-smile that made her lips tingle with the desire to kiss him.

She couldn't lie to herself anymore. She was attracted to Kade.

A tentacle of fear slid around her body, locking her in a strangling grip. This couldn't be happening, and yet it was. Lexie struggled to keep her composure as Kade stopped two feet from her.

"You want a hint?"

Not trusting her voice right then, she just nodded.

"It's a pretty boring story, really. It involves youthful stupidity, a bulldog, and an old Buick. And that's all I can tell you right now."

His gaze lowered to her mouth, and Lexie saw a small muscle in his jaw flex. When his eyes returned to hers, a spark of heat flared in them before he smiled.

"I know this is wrong for many reasons, but I'm attracted to you. You want to know why I never hung around when you were with Jason? I—I—thought you were so hot, and I'd never wanted one of Jason's girlfriends before." He rushed ahead when she opened her mouth to protest. "I would like to spend time with you."

Lexie needed clarification. "Spend time with me? Exactly what does that mean?"

Kade gave her a half smile. "Casual dating and see where that leads. Have dinner, go to the movies…that kind of stuff. You don't have to answer right now. Take some time to think about it."

Kade placed his hand against her neck. Her brain screamed at her to flee, but her body had other ideas. As Kade's fingers grazed her skin, goose bumps ran down her back. The heat she'd glimpsed in his eyes before returned and intensified. His gaze dropped to her mouth again, and she knew he wanted to kiss her.

Anxiety turned her breathing shallow when she realized that she wanted to kiss Kade, too. It had been so long since she'd kissed a man that she felt starved for just that simple contact.

With a start, she realized she'd never kissed anyone other than Jason since they'd started dating.

Glancing at Kade's sensual mouth, she wondered what kissing him would feel like.

He inched closer and lowered his head. Lexie's eyes closed as his lips settled over hers.

Lexie stiffened when she felt Kade's arm slide around her waist and pull her into contact with his body. Of their own accord, her hands lifted to rest against his chest, and his hard muscles instantly fascinated her. He slanted his mouth over hers and parted his lips, and it was like somewhere inside the dam holding back her emotions blew her to smithereens.

Winding her arms around his neck, Lexie opened to him and met his gently questing tongue with hers. She expected him to deepen the kiss, but he teased her, flicking his tongue against hers while sliding his fingers into her hair. Lexie started spiraling down into desire, and she wanted more.

Leaning harder into him, she raised up on her toes and intensified the kiss, thrilling to the way his hard torso felt against her breasts. A whimper rose in her throat when he wrapped his arms around her and answered her demand.

A large car engine started somewhere near them, startling Lexie. She gasped and broke away from Kade, looking around wildly for the car. A silver Charger backed up, and her heart sank. Zip. He must've been heading off to the bar after working late. Maybe he hadn't seen them kissing.

Lexie pushed against Kade's chest, and he released her. As Zip headed out of the parking lot, he grinned over at them from behind the wheel, and Lexie's cheeks burned when he gave them a jaunty little wave and drove off.

Groaning, Lexie put a hand to her forehead. "Oh, God. This is bad. Zip doesn't have much of a filter and he can't keep a secret to save his life."

Kade chuckled at her embarrassment. "Who cares if he saw us? I don't." He gathered her close again. "Now, where were we?"

Anger flashed through Lexie. What the hell was she thinking? She extricated herself from his embrace and put distance between them. "I care very much. This could get me fired if Marcus finds out." Looking at him, Lexie cursed him for being so sexy. It was almost impossible to resist kissing him again. "If he thinks this will interfere with my job, I'm toast."

A fierce scowl settled on Kade's face, and he grew even sexier to Lexie. "You let me know if he does and I'll deal with him."

His protective attitude touched Lexie, but she didn't want him getting into a fight with Marcus or Tom. "No, I'll handle it. I can take care of myself." Regret settled in her stomach. "Kade, I just can't do this. What about Jason?"

"I thought you were divorcing him."

"I am, but he's going through so much and if either of us are to gain his trust to get him into rehab… It won't work if he thinks we've both betrayed him."

Taking her hand, he raised it to his lips, pressing a kiss to the back of her knuckles. "I can wait. I can wait until we've sorted out the situation with Jason. Just don't shut me out. And when we find Jason, once he's out of rehab, I'm going to be honest. I'll tell him how I feel. I won't walk away this time."

She remembered Jason's warning to stay away from Kade on the phone call. "I think he's already guessed."

"I wonder why Jason is so worried about us? Does he think

you have feelings for me?" He kissed her hand again. "No answer to that? Goodnight, Lex. Sweet dreams."

He moved back from her when everything inside her wanted to pull him close. Forcing herself to walk to her car, she looked up as Kade tossed her a smile before he got behind the wheel and drove off without a backward glance.

What a bloody mess. Why did she feel so guilty when her husband had stolen from her, spent their money on drugs and dicked around on her? All she'd done was crush on his sexy older brother.

She'd go to hell for sure. Jason would want to send her there.

She straightened her shoulders. Jason had lost the right to have a say in anything she did.

She wanted Kade, and she refused to feel guilty about that.

Well, just a bit.

She was about to start her car when the door to the showroom opened, silhouetting two people in the doorway. She watched as a woman reached up and tenderly cupped the man's face as she leaned in and kissed him. For a moment, she thought Tom must be here with Kendra, but then the woman stepped into the beam from the security light.

Lexie held in a gasp. Stella! Who was she kissing?

But she knew the answer long before he pulled the door closed, and after locking it, he too stepped into the light. Marcus.

Like a stunned mullet, she sat there and watched as they walked hand in hand, kissing and cuddling to Stella's car parked out on the street.

How long had this been going on and did Kendra know? It looked like more than a causal hook up. They looked like a comfortable couple out for the evening. Besides, if it was a casual hook up, they wouldn't hide it. Stella would share all the juicy details with her.

Kendra would freak if she knew her best friend, Stella, was having a—what, exactly?—with her brother. Kendra was protective of Marcus after all he'd been through since the crash. But

Marcus was a real horn dog, a different woman every night. Maybe he'd met his match in Stella. Stella was Kendra's best friend, but she was as bad as Marcus. Stella was known as a definite love them and leave them kind of woman. Kendra wouldn't want her brother hurt.

She missed her two girlfriends. Lexie had been moping over Jason too long. She hadn't had a girls' night with Kendra and Stella for ages. Not since little Matti was born.

She slid down in her seat so they wouldn't see her. She would keep her secret to herself, but it didn't mean she couldn't wheedle the truth from Stella over a few drinks. Was this a casual hook up or was this something more?

Chapter Eight

Sitting in the lunchroom the next day, Lexie sketched with one hand and held a ham and swiss sandwich in the other. This was often the way she spent her lunch hour. During the morning, design ideas swirled in her brain, but usually they solidified into concrete concepts by noon and it was imperative to complete a rough draft while the images were fresh in her mind.

Taking a bite of her sandwich, she glanced up to find Tom giving her a speculative glance from where he stood by the refrigerator. "What?" she demanded.

Tom shrugged and opened the fridge. "Nothing."

Lexie narrowed her eyes as she chewed and returned her attention to her work. In a few moments, Tom sat down next to her. Looking at him, Lexie saw curiosity in her friend's eyes and knew exactly what was on his mind. With an inward groan, she placed her sandwich on a paper plate and wiped her hands on a napkin.

"Okay. Let's get this over with," she said.

If she hadn't known Tom better, she would've bought his look of innocence. "Get what over with?"

"You want to know what happened last night with Kade,

right?" Lexie had gotten through the morning with no one mentioning her kiss with Kade. Zip had kept his mouth shut after all, and she felt bad for doubting him.

Tom gave a brief nod. "It *had* crossed my mind."

After taking a sip of her iced tea, Lexie simply said, "We had a nice dinner, then he dropped me off here and I went home." She didn't feel one iota of guilt over not telling Tom the full story. She wasn't ready to divulge that information yet because she was still too confused, and she needed time to think about it.

Tom's dark blond eyebrows drew together. "That's it?"

Irked, Lexie said, "Yeah. What were you expecting to happen?" She pointed at Tom. "If you say you thought I'd sleep with Kade, I'll wreck your face."

"No, of course not. Although it would be no one's business but your own."

Lexie played with the button on the right sleeve of her overalls. She knew that Kade's choice for their meal was odd, but it had shown her a softer side of him, and she loved how he helped out. He'd been right about her needing something else to focus on. Seeing how poor some of those people were, how they'd lost everything, made her grateful for what she had. Especially her job and friends.

"I'm really thankful to you for everything. I might've been out on the street if it wasn't for you."

Tom laid a hand on her forearm. "You know I'll always help you, Lex. I'd never let you be homeless."

"You've done so much for me," she responded. "You hired me against Marcus' wishes—"

"You kind of hired yourself, as I recall," Tom interjected.

Lexie smiled sheepishly. "Technically, Sully did that, so it wasn't all my doing. Thanks for having my back."

Tom pulled her into a one-armed hug. "No thanks needed." He released her. "So, how are things going with Kade's car?"

"Great. I finalized the design and I'm just waiting for Zip to finish all the welding, so I can install the new carpeting that came in this morning," Lexie replied.

Tom stood and patted her shoulder. "Good work. I can't wait to see it when you're done."

She smiled as he walked away and then returned to her sketching. Kade's image rose in her mind, and she wondered what he was doing. Was he writing? Lexie couldn't picture him sitting behind a computer because he didn't look the part of a journalist. She found the incongruity of Kade's chosen profession and his appearance fascinating.

Looking down at her sketch pad, she resisted the impulse to draw Kade. She'd be mortified if anyone ever saw it, especially Kade.

Her cellphone alarm went off, meaning lunchtime was over.

Lexie was glad for the interruption because it kept her from doing something stupid, like calling him. She gathered up her things, threw away her garbage, and went to the locker room. Once her belongings were stowed in her locker, she hurried out to the garage.

Entering her bay area, she found Zip hard at work installing the new floor in the Alfa. Sparks flew as he welded the custom-made piece of steel he'd fashioned to the underside of the car. Since she couldn't work on the Alfa right then, she checked on some part orders she'd placed and tried to put Kade out of her mind.

Just then, Marcus walked past, and she hugged her secret to herself.

"What's that smile for?" he asked.

"Nothing, just thinking about a joke Zip told me earlier."

Marcus kept walking, and she reminded herself to ring Stella later.

Queen's "We Will Rock You" shattered the silence, jerking Lexie from slumber. She fumbled around on her nightstand until she located the offensive device and squinted at the screen which displayed Kade's number. She caught sight of the time as she hit the answer button.

"Why the hell are you calling me at five-thirty a.m.?"

His slightly hoarse laugh sent a jolt of desire down her spine, and Lexie was suddenly wide awake. "I thought I'd take you to breakfast before I head to the gym."

The memory of their kiss from the other night was never far from her mind, and his voice brought it into sharp focus. His warm, supple lips on hers, the way he'd tasted, the heat of his muscular body against her palms. Her breathing grew shallower as she recalled how good it had felt to have a man's arms around her again.

"Did you fall back to sleep?"

At Kade's question, Lexie flipped over onto her back with an exasperated sigh. "No. There's no danger of that now. Once I'm awake, there's no going back."

"Sorry. I know a place that has the fluffiest pancakes you've ever tasted and nice crispy, salty bacon, and killer coffee. C'mon, Lexie. It's just breakfast. Besides, I can update you on what my team has found out on Jason."

Lexie's stomach growled at the mention of bacon, one of her favorite foods. It didn't matter what time of day or night it was, Lexie was always eager to consume the artery-clogging meat.

Her ravenous stomach shouted at her to accept his invitation. "Okay, if you're buying."

"I am. Meet me at Sunny's on Bartlett Street in half an hour. See ya."

Getting out of bed, Lexie felt a little giddy at the thought of a free breakfast. She raced through showering and threw on a pair of jeans shorts and a Joan Jett & the Blackhearts t-shirt. As she pulled her damp hair into a high ponytail to air dry, she caught sight of her reflection in her bathroom mirror and paused.

The woman she saw staring back at her looked different. Instead of the shadow of sadness that seemed to be ever present in her eyes, there was a little sparkle in their dark depths. It confused her because nothing in her life had changed to cause it.

Or had it?

Kade.

Lexie shied away from attributing the lift in her spirits to him, instead giving the credit to time. It was supposed to be the healer of all wounds, right? She told herself that Kade's appearance in her life right then was nothing more than a coincidence. That decided, she grabbed her backpack and keys on the way out the door.

Chapter Nine

K ade sat in a booth by the window, sipping water and working on an article while he waited for Lexie. From his vantage point, he'd be able to see her as soon as she arrived. Calling Lexie had been a gamble, but he'd hoped she could be enticed with food. He was glad he'd taken the chance.

Three mornings each week, he boxed at the Golden Gloves Gym and always ate a light breakfast at Sunny's beforehand. Kade never wasted time, and he often worked while he waited for his meals. He'd just started making notes for his weekly blog when Lexie walked in the door and looked around.

She looked gorgeous and adorable at the same time. Her ponytail was a little unruly, cascading down her back in a thick mass of sable waves. He stifled a groan at the way her jeans shorts molded to her hips and showed off her up-to-her-armpits sexy legs. How his brother could've ever cheated on her...

That's what addiction did to you. Kade knew if he was ever lucky enough to make Lexie his, he'd never want another woman again.

He got her attention with a brief wave and closed his Surface Pro. Since he'd gotten Lexie out of bed, he felt that he owed her his full attention, not that he'd be able to concentrate on work with her around, anyway.

Her smile as she walked towards his table was a trifle sleepy, and Kade imagined what she looked like upon first waking in the morning. His writer's imagination kicked in, and he saw them lying in bed together in a tangle of arms and legs. He could almost feel how soft and warm she'd be against his body.

Snapping out of the fantasy as Lexie reached his table, Kade said, "Good morning, Lex."

She slid into the booth opposite him and smothered a yawn with a hand. "Morning. I need coffee."

"That can be arranged." Kade motioned to a waitress. "I'm glad you came."

Lexie smiled and picked up one of the laminated menus. "I didn't have any choice once my belly heard the word 'bacon.' I'm surprised you didn't hear it rumble over the phone."

Kade chuckled as the waitress arrived.

"What can I get you?" she asked.

Kade motioned for Lexie to give her order and listened with amusement as she ordered a huge breakfast of pancakes, eggs, bacon, and fresh fruit. He chose whole wheat pancakes, turkey sausage, fruit and one egg. Lexie accepted the mug of coffee the waitress offered, but Kade declined.

Lexie sent him a curious look as she put cream and sugar in her drink. "Don't you like coffee?"

"I love it, but not right before working out. It's a diuretic, and I need lots of hydration," he replied. "But when I'm on a deadline and have to write all night, I drink tons of it."

A smile accompanied a shake of Lexie's head. "If I didn't know you, I'd never take you for a writer."

He laughed because he heard that a lot, but he wanted to know why she felt that way. "Why?"

She brought her ponytail around to drape over her chest and played with the curly strands of hair at the end. "I don't know. I guess I think of writers as geeky people who don't go out of their houses much." Her eyes traveled over him. "And there's nothing geeky about you. I mean, look at you. You look like a sexier Vin Diesel—all fast and furious—okay, no furious, actually. You smile too much."

Kade's shoulders shook with laughter and she grinned at him. "I've never heard anyone describe me that way before, but I'm glad you think I'm sexy."

Her cheeks turned pink, and she rubbed her forehead. "Sorry. I never know what's going to come out of my mouth at this time of day."

"No need to apologize. Compliments are always welcome, especially from you." He put his elbows on the table and leaned closer. "You know what I can't figure out?"

Lexie sipped her coffee. "What's that?"

Kade decided to push his luck and take another risk. "Why I let Jason marry you."

Lexie's blush deepened, and she set her mug on the table. "Quite frankly, looking back, I wished you'd stopped me marrying him, too." She almost cringed at the bitterness in her voice.

Kade's teeth ground together in anger at the way her voice went a little flat, and he put a hand over hers. "My brother is sick, Lexie. It's not my fault, and it's not yours. Don't let him make you feel less than you are."

Although she glanced at his hand, Lexie didn't pull away from him and his chest puffed out. "It's hard when he treated me like shit. It's hard to walk in on Jason in our bed with some track bunny and not take it personally."

"That says more about Jason than you."

Her beautiful eyes welled with tears. "That makes me stupid and gullible."

"No. Not only are you beautiful as hell, you're way smarter and more mature than he'll ever be. You have an incredible work ethic, you're a phenomenal artist and killer mechanic. Any man would be lucky to have you, and I know it doesn't feel like it right now, but you're so much better off without Jason the addict. You deserve someone who'll appreciate all your fine qualities."

Lexie arched an eyebrow but still didn't pull her hand from his. "Someone like you, you mean?"

Kade gave her a curt nod. "Yeah, maybe. Like I said, that's up to you. But even if it's not with me, I hope you find happiness again with a guy who sees all those wonderful things about you."

She stared at him like a deer in headlights, and he could see she was about to run. He'd pushed too hard.

Lexie rose and flapped a funny little wave in his direction as she made for the door with quick strides.

Kade sighed as he shoved his computer in its case and followed her. She was already out the door, and he rushed to catch her before she could start her Jeep. She was just getting into it when he caught up to her.

"Lexie, wait." He put a hand on her shoulder. "I'm sorry. But I won't lie or pretend. Not with you."

Lexie whirled around, fear and anger shining in her eyes. "There's nothing to talk about, Kade. I can't do this. I'm not ready, and even if I was, you're the last guy I'd get involved with. I know it's stupid but I feel guilty. Your Jason's brother."

Dismay made his stomach drop even though he understood.

He wasn't about to give up, though. "I'll wait."

Lexie ground her teeth together. "What if we got together? The past would always be there between us all. Jason would be there. Do you see how awkward it would be?"

Kade replied, "Only if we let it. Look, Jason's had his chance. Both of us deserve to be happy, and I believe we can make each *other* happy. For all you know, once Jason's clean, he might agree we should be together."

"Kade, what if he's not? I couldn't stand knowing that I caused a rift between you guys. I'd always feel guilty about it."

His mouth twisted in a wry smile. "You have anyway. I can't simply turn these feelings off."

Lexie played with the steering wheel while she mulled over his words. She blinked in confusion a few times as she gazed up at him. Once again, he wished they could find Jason and get this situation sorted. The longer it dragged on, the more likely it was she'd freeze him out.

"What do you want from me, Kade?"

Kade gave her a playful smile. "Right now, I just want you to come back inside and have breakfast with me."

Lexie's brows puckered. "That's it? Just have breakfast?"

He put a hand to his chest. "I promise. I'm starving, and I'd like your company while I eat. They have great bacon here, remember? Plus, I have news about my brother."

He hoped his teasing smile and coaxing made it impossible for Lexie to resist him.

She chuckled and shook her head. "That's culinary blackmail."

His smile broadened. "Whatever it takes. C'mon. I know you're hungry, and you've got a full day ahead of you of fixing my jalopy. Better fuel up."

Lexie smirked at his bad pun. "Very funny."

"So, what'll it be? Leaving with an empty stomach or filling up on pancakes and bacon and coffee…"

"Okay, okay," she interjected. "Let's go eat."

Kade rubbed his hands together. "Now you're talking."

He motioned for Lexie to precede him back into the diner, and Lexie laughed as she reentered the restaurant. They took their previous booth and their waitress came to top off Lexie's coffee.

"Tell me about Jason. My P.I. has nothing."

Kade put down his fork. "My team caught a break. They found an old girlfriend, and she told them Jason had stopped by. Apparently, he was talking about checking into rehab, but she doesn't know which one."

Lexie clapped her hands. "That's great news all around. Jason gets help, and there can't be too many rehabs in Chicago to check."

"If it's a rehab in Chicago. He could have gone anywhere."

She shrugged and drank her coffee. "How many rehabs in the USA can there be?"

"You'd be surprised—thousands. And with confidentiality top of their list, finding him may take some time." Kade didn't want to burst her bubble. Jason could have been lying to the girl. He might not be in rehab at all. Lexie, once again believed the best in everyone—even Jason, who she shouldn't trust with a ten-foot pole.

"I have a good feeling about this. Come on, let's eat. The food better be as good as you say it is," she grumbled good-naturedly.

"Trust me. It is."

She speared him with mock-fierce look. "We'll just see about that."

Kade laughed and took a swallow of his water.

Forty-five minutes later, Lexie's stomach hurt from laughing at the funny childhood stories Kade told her. They were so amusing that she didn't mind that they included Jason. They reminded her of the Jason she'd fallen in love with—before he'd got hooked on coke.

"Needless to say, I got spanked over that one," he concluded the current story.

Lexie held a hand to her abdomen. "I'm not surprised. I would've killed you for putting Comet and dishwashing liquid all over the kitchen floor."

Kade made a placating gesture. "I thought I was helping Mom clean."

"In the middle of the night?"

"I was only seven. Give me a break."

Lexie chuckled as she thought of her ex-mother-in-law. "I can just imagine Jackie's face when she came downstairs in the morning and found all that goop dried on the linoleum."

"She hit the roof, and Dad turned my butt red in a hurry. I never tried to clean again," Kade said.

Lexie jumped when the alarm on her cellphone went off. Several other patrons in the diner glanced at her while she stabbed at the dismiss button. "Sorry about that," she said.

"Is seven a.m. your normal wake-up time?" Kade asked.

Lexie brought up her work email account on her phone to check on the status of a couple of the parts orders she had placed for Kade's car. "Yeah. Why?"

Kade smiled. "I'll keep that in mind for next time."

Lexie's eyebrows lifted. "Next time?"

"Yeah." Kade snatched the check.

"Kade, I can pay for my breakfast," Lexie protested.

"No, no. I promised to pay, so I am. No arguing." He sobered a little. "I really enjoyed myself."

"Me too," Lexie said, meaning it. "I'm glad you invited me, even if you woke me up. The bacon made up for it."

Kade grinned. "I knew it would. Well, I guess I'd better get to the gym and let you do whatever you do before work."

He got out of the booth, and Lexie followed. "It just depends on my mood. Usually, I go for a run, but I think I'll skip that this morning. I'm too full."

Kade went to the register, paid the bill and returned to Lexie. "Maybe we could go for a run together sometime," he suggested as they started for the door.

Sudden nerves made Lexie's stomach sour a little. "Maybe." She quashed her needless uneasiness. "We'll see." She flicked a coy smile at Kade before going out the door.

It surprised her when he followed her to her car.

"Are you afraid you won't be able to keep up with me?"

His challenging question made her turn around and arch an eyebrow. "Are you trying to bait me into running with you?"

"Is it working?"

Lexie crossed her arms over her chest. "Nope."

"You sure?"

"Positive."

Kade held up a surrendering hand. "Okay, but let me know if you change your mind."

Her eyes widened when Kade leaned towards her. She froze as his lips grazed her cheek. The faint scents of citrus and syrup reached her, making her hungry for something other than food.

As Kade straightened, their gazes collided and held for what seemed like long moments. She caught his minute glance at her mouth, and her brain screamed, *Kiss me!* Her breathing became shallow, and she stomped on the caution that tried to rise to the surface.

Fisting her fingers in Kade's gray t-shirt, she hauled him against her and pressed her mouth to his.

She let out a surprised moan when he instantly responded. His hand settled on her right hip as she ran the tip of her tongue over his bottom lip. Suddenly, it felt like it was a hundred degrees out when he delved his tongue into her mouth. Winding an arm around his neck, Lexie pressed against his broad chest. The contact made her nipples grow taut.

Kade's fingers dug into her flesh a little as the kiss intensified, sending a thrill through her. She wanted to lose herself in him, to feel desired as she hadn't in so long. She moved her hand up the back of his neck, liking the feel of his smooth-skinned head, and an intense urge to explore the rest of him washed over her.

Fire lit inside Lexie as he plundered her mouth, the heady taste of him making her almost drunk with lust—no, it was more than that. Hell yeah, she wanted him. She should let him go, but she let herself linger a few more moments, enjoying the feel of his stubble against her chin.

"Hey! Get a room, you two!"

Kade jerked, breaking contact with Lexie and banging his

head on the car roof. A giggle escaped her lips, partly to cover her embarrassment. What must he think? She was definitely sending him mixed signals.

He grinned as he pointed his hand in the general direction of the male voice that had shouted at them and flipped the guy off. "Sounds like someone's jealous," he remarked.

"I guess so." Lexie cleared her throat when she heard a breathy note in her voice. She didn't want him to know how much he affected her. "Thanks for breakfast."

"You're welcome."

Lexie resisted looking at Kade's mouth because she was afraid that she'd kiss him again. They'd already put on enough of a public show, thanks to her. "Well, I better get to work."

Kade brushed a kiss to her cheek and withdrew. "Okay. Have a good day." His smile caused her pulse to falter. "I'll be in touch about the car... and other things, too." He winked and turned away from her.

She admired the view as he walked to his car. If his ass looked that good in jeans, she could imagine how much better it was when he was naked. Realizing she was staring, Lexie admonished herself and started her car.

Kade looked back at her, and she waved at him before leaving. Lexie's insides jangled as she drove. She hadn't had the desire to kiss a man in a long time.

For six months, she'd fended off numerous passes and turned down dates, except Pace's. The dinner had been nice, but no spark. She'd had fun, but she'd had no desire to jump Pace's bones as he kissed her good night. Pace was now firmly in the friend zone, more like an older brother. And he'd headed back to Europe yesterday. So what made Kade different?

And why did it have to be her ex-brother-in-law who piqued her interest?

Lexie groaned and almost banged her head on the steering wheel. Then she saw that the clock on the dash read seven-fifteen a.m., and she turned her mind to the thing she understood the most—work.

"Get your rear in gear," she muttered.

With a huge breath to clear her jumbled mind, Lexie headed for work and an Alfa that needed some final touches.

Chapter Ten

Sitting in the lunchroom, Lexie tried to concentrate on drawing up a preliminary design sketch for a new customer, but it was tough going. She hadn't heard from Kade for two days, which was odd.

Suspicion crowded her brain, making her temple ache. Had Kade found Jason? But why would he hide that from her? She dismissed that idea because it didn't square with what she knew of Kade.

Besides, Sully was a great judge of character, so his approval of Kade went a long way with Lexie. She chided herself for acting like a teenager with a crush. Jason had once told her that Kade always retreated from the world when he was writing a big article, or if he was on a tight book deadline. Most likely, that's what had happened.

Lexie glanced at her cellphone sitting on the table next to her. She tapped the end of her pencil against her lips as she contemplated texting Kade. Images of their fiery embrace the other day danced in her mind. Kade's thorough exploration of her mouth had left her aching for more.

Her temperature started rising as she remembered Kade sliding his arm around her waist, hauling her against his chest.

She chuckled about being shouted at by that guy and at Kade's reaction.

It was a good thing they'd stopped because Kade's growing arousal beckoned. Damn, but she'd almost reached down to caress him through his jeans.

Her smile broadened. It felt good knowing that she still had that effect on a man. Jason's cruel words and lack of interest had dented her confidence in the bedroom.

She sighed as she gazed once more at her cellphone, as though it could help her decide whether to send Kade a message. Before she chickened out, she snatched the phone up, found Kade in her contacts and hit the call button.

K ade had been up most of the night again, and it seemed like he'd just gotten to sleep when his phone rang. Growling at the intrusion, he fumbled around for it on his nightstand, but it wasn't there. Rolling over, he spotted it on the floor near the bed. He grabbed it, and woke up fast when he saw Lexie's name on the caller ID.

"You're up early," he greeted her. Her answering chuckle made him smile.

"I'm taking you up on the offer of going for a run."

Kade rolled over and sat up on the side of the bed. Looking at the phone, he saw that it was close to noon. He yawned as he realized that he'd slept for six hours. Rubbing his eyes, he asked, "Now? Aren't you at work?"

Lexie laughed. "Not now. Tomorrow morning."

Kade stifled a groan. He was still on a strict deadline and would most likely have to pull another all-nighter. However, he would not turn down the chance to spend time with Lexie.

"Sounds great. Where do you want to meet?"

"Have you ever done the West Loop at Elysian Park?"

"No. I hear it's nice, though. Easy, but nice."

"Not the way I do it. Meet me there tomorrow at five-thirty. Bye."

The way she'd left him no choice but to go amused Kade. Lexie's moxie was one thing he most admired about her. With a grin, he fell back into bed. He reset his alarm for three p.m. He had a long night of writing ahead of him before his run.

Kade could see Lexie doing warm-up stretches while she waited for him as he drove up the next morning. She was as flexible as fuck, and naughty thoughts jumped into his brain. She grabbed her right ankle and brought it up behind her, and all he could think about was what those legs would feel like wrapped around his waist.

The sun's early rays shone down on the dirt parking lot, turning it and everything else it touched to burnished gold. He hoped it wouldn't get too hot before the run was over, or his lack of sleep might see him throw up if they ran too far.

He parked the Mercedes and jumped out. "Morning, Lex. You look more awake than the other morning."

His blood turned hot as he took in the sight of Lexie in a pair of thigh-length, skin-tight purple running shorts and a matching sports bra. He'd seen her in a bikini a few times and knew she had a sexy, toned body, but she looked even better than he remembered. Her shapely, long legs and slightly defined midsection led up to the swell of her breasts, which in his estimation were the perfect size, just large enough to fill his palms.

Get a grip, he thought as his groin tightened with a small influx of heated blood. His sweat shorts weren't great camouflage for an erection, so he focused on her eyes. The sun had turned them a warm coffee brown, and he loved the way her smile made them sparkle.

"That's right. I'm bright-eyed and bushy-tailed and ready to kick your ass."

Kade grinned as he stretched. "We'll see about that."

"Mmm hmm. I'm ready to go, so hurry with those stretches. Daylight's burning."

"You sound like an eighties military movie," Kade said as he started a series of walking lunges. He loved how Lexie watched every move.

"Okay. Ready to do this?"

Kade's question snapped Lexie out of her thoughts and she nodded. "Ready."

He gestured toward the trail. "Lead on."

F orty-five minutes later, they reached the pinnacle of the one steep dirt trail. Even though Kade was in excellent condition, he was still sweating and huffing and puffing from the run Lexie had just put him through. She'd eschewed the easier sections of the trail in favor of the demanding parts. On the wider, safer trails, she'd challenged him to turn around and run backwards, and his thighs burned from the unfamiliar exercise.

"Don't tell the guys you whipped my ass up that last steep incline, I'll never hear the end of it," he panted, sucking in large gulps of air.

Even leaning over, her hands on her thighs and dripping with sweat, Lexie looked as sexy as hell. How ironic that he didn't have the strength to flirt with her. His legs were shaking like jelly. A wasted opportunity given they were alone, on a mountain, with the most stunning view all around.

She shot him a beaming smile at his inferred compliment. "None of the guys can beat me up this hill."

His body tightened, and not from the screaming muscles. Disappointment flooded his body. Had she brought other guys up here? "You bring all your boyfriends up here?"

Her face heated, and she gave him her back. "The view up here is amazing," she said, ignoring his question.

His eyes flicked to the city below, but not for long before they were back gazing at the best view—Lexie.

Speaking of stunning, Lexie, all hot and bothered didn't help slow his pounding heart. What that girl did to him… if he had the energy, he'd pull her into his arms and…

Maybe not. His legs shook with the effort to remain standing.

He did, however, have the energy to pull off his tank top and wipe his face and neck. Pride came rushing back when he caught Lexie's eyes following his movements, filled with appreciation and hunger. He raised his arms above his head and stretched. He shot her another quick look. Yup. He loved that she was admiring him more than the city vista below.

To have her look at him with such sensual hunger, he'd eagerly do this run all over again if he had to. He turned and looked at the city below.

The sun seemed to hold the smog at bay, and the LA skyscrapers stood out against the clear blue sky. Dodger Stadium, other tourist spots, and neighborhoods were visible, but what impressed Kade the most was that if he kept his perusal to the more immediate surroundings, he could almost believe that he lived in a less urban city.

Hundreds of trees, shrubs, and flowers filled the park, through which numerous running and hiking trails and foot-paths wound. Many varieties of birds made their homes there, and he'd seen a few rabbits. He'd lived in LA a long time, and he wondered why he'd never visited Elysian Park before now.

"It's beautiful here. Like a forest oasis away from the city," he commented.

Lexie moved to stand beside him, also gazing at the splendor before her. "I come here a lot to run and clear my head. It's a great place to watch the sunrise or sunset. It's good for my soul, I guess you'd say."

"I can see why." He looked down at her. "Thanks for showing me a little of your world."

"You're welcome." She clapped her hands together. "Okay. Rest time is over. Time to head back."

Kade tied his sweaty tank around his waist. "All right. First one to the bottom has to buy breakfast tomorrow. Deal?"

Lexie rose to his challenge. "Deal," she agreed and sprinted off.

Grinning, Kade watched her go, taking a few moments to admire her. He didn't wait long, though, because he didn't want her to think he was giving her a head start. Lexie was the kind of woman who wanted to earn things on merit.

So, he chased after Lexie, catching up with her. She was moving at a fast clip, but Kade knew she could go much faster. He recognized her tactic; conserve energy so she could make a move for it later. Matching his strides with hers, Kade let her set the pace, content to do the same thing.

The whole way down the path, they kept pace with each other, biding their time. Lexie pointed out other good trails, and they chitchatted a little about Kade's car. When they had about a quarter of the way to go, Lexie decided it was time to leave Kade in the dust. She gathered herself and shot ahead. Her legs working like pistons, propelling her forward.

Kade inwardly chuckled, not letting her get ahead. He saw her understand that he wouldn't hand her victory. Deciding to go for it, she ran flat out, redoubling her efforts, but Kade pulled ahead. He watched her eyes narrow as she drew even with him and stayed there for several strides before he left her behind again.

He reached her Jeep, which was closer, and came to a halt beside it. Would she be a sore loser?

Kade held out a fist to her. "Good run. You got some speed, woman."

With a smile, Lexie bumped her fist against his and, to his delight, stared at his glistening chest as it rose and fell with his rapid breathing. "I do all right."

He took the tank top from around his midsection and wiped

his face. "You do a lot better than *all right*. You run faster than a lot of guys I know."

"Thanks. I'll get you next time."

Next time? Joy almost choked him She wanted to do this again? "Name the place and time."

Still puffing, she said, "I'd rather buy you breakfast. Tomorrow morning at the diner?"

Kade nodded. "It must be early like the other day, since I have training, though. Is that okay?"

"Sure. No problem."

"Great."

Without giving her time to think, Kade closed the distance between them. Heat flared in her smiling eyes as he rested a hand on her shoulder. Her lips parted a few fractions when he slid his hand up her neck and pulled her towards him. For a fleeting moment before he pressed his mouth to hers, he wondered what it would be like to kiss her whenever he wanted, every day of the year.

A thrill ran through him at the idea of making Lexie his. He urged her even closer as the kiss deepened. Her bare stomach contacted his, and he groaned low in his throat.

Not the time or place for this. So the next moment, Kade slowed things down. He desperately wanted to get her alone, away from public eyes. He didn't know how he'd achieve that.

She stepped back and yelped when her side-view mirror hit her between her shoulder blades. "Ow! Shit!"

"Are you okay?" Kade asked.

Lexie waved away his concern. "Yeah, I'm fine. Just didn't realize how close I was to my car."

A knowing smile curved his mouth. "I know how you feel. I kinda forgot where we were—again."

Kade thought Christmas had arrived as she trailed an index finger down his chest, stopping just short of his navel. His erection would soon be clear for all to see, but he just couldn't seem to care.

"Maybe someday we'll be at the right place at the right time."

Kade's eyebrows rose. Had she just said that? It was as if she'd read his thoughts. It gave him hope that there might be a future for them, but he cautioned himself about pressing too hard. "Maybe we will."

Their gazes locked and held for several moments before Lexie looked away. "I better get going so I'm not late for work."

Kade nodded. "Yeah. I don't want you to get in trouble with Marcus."

"Right. Thanks for the run. I had a good time."

"Me too. A really good time."

They said goodbye and Kade watched her drive away.

Idiot. You should have asked her to your place for dinner. She all but offered to be alone with him.

Now his erection was there for good. One thought of having Lexie in his bed meant it would be a painful ride home to take an ice-cold shower.

Chapter Eleven

Girls' night, and she couldn't wait. She was having a night on the town with Kendra and Stella. Tom was babysitting, and they'd decided on grabbing a meal at Kendra's favorite Italian restaurant near where Kendra lived.

Lexie couldn't afford the Uber, so Kendra had picked her up. Stella was already at the table when they arrived, with a bottle of bubbles sitting in an ice bucket.

"Are we celebrating?" she asked as she sat down and picked up a menu.

"Are we?" Kendra said with a wink, while Stella giggled.

She looked at Stella. "Have you already drunk a bottle?"

More giggling. "I heard there might be something to celebrate."

She looked at Kendra's knowing smile and secretly cursed Tom. He'd been blabbing. "If you are referring to finding Jason, then no. Nothing yet."

"She was referring to your dates with Kade," Stella replied. "We know all about the dinner, and I've heard a few breakfasts, too."

"And who did you hear that from, Stella? Marcus, by any

chance?" Time to turn the tables. She watched as Stella's smile faded, and her face turned red.

Stella looked at Kendra. "I'm sure Kendra told me."

"I only knew about the dinner, not the breakfast. Who told you about that?"

Stella looked at the table. "Must have been Tom."

Kendra's eyes were grilling Stella. "I wonder why he didn't tell *me*."

Lexie felt terrible. Stella's body language stated she didn't want them to know about her and Marcus.

"Anyway, I'll only celebrate when Jason's found. But I'd love a glass of bubbles." She reached for her glass.

"So, no more news?" Kendra reached out and patted her hand. "Kade will find him. He might not like how Jason's behaving, but he *is* his brother and he loves him."

"I have my P.I. looking for him, too, but I'm running out of money and time. Two weeks—"

"What do you mean, running out of time?"

Whoops. "Promise me not to get mad or judgmental?" They both nodded. "Jason fraudulently mortgaged my cabin at Clear Lake and then took off with the money. I didn't know, so I made no mortgage payments. The bank is foreclosing in three weeks if I don't come up with the nine months of back payments."

"Bastard. Ooh, and here I was feeling sorry for Jason and his addiction, but shit, that is low." Stella opened her purse and took out her checkbook. "You are not losing that cabin. I know how much it means to you. How much is the loan? You can pay me back little by little. I have more money than I'll ever need in a lifetime."

Tears welled in her eyes. Stella's father was a movie producer, and she had a trust fund the size of Fort Knox. "That's so kind, but Kade has it covered if we don't find Jason in time, or if the money is gone when we do."

"Interesting. You'll take money from Kade, but not Stella."

She shrugged at Kendra's statement. "He's a Colter. And a

Colter owes me. Besides, he's thankful I didn't report Jason to the police."

"And you're happy with taking Kade's money?"

Stella knew how to rub it in. "I'm not happy taking *anyone's* money, but I won't lose that cabin. Not when I've done nothing wrong."

The "but you were the one stupid enough to marry Jason," hung in the air.

"At least there's one decent Colter."

She agreed with Kendra's sentiment. Kade was a good guy—so far. "I just hate that Kade's got to clean up Jason's mess. And I must let him because Jason's probably sniffed the money up his nose."

"I suspect he's used to it. Jason's been the problem younger brother all his life."

Stella would know, she'd grown up in the same privileged crowd in LA. Lexie had only walked into it when she'd scored a job on the racing circuit and she'd stupidly fallen under the spell of flashy cars and loads of money. All the wealth and fun and carefreeness—she was like a kid in a candy store. Perhaps if she'd grown up with friends like Kendra and Stella, she wouldn't have been blinded by the trappings of wealth.

"So what exactly is the situation with Kade. Are you dating? Or have you merely come together because of the need to find Jason?"

There's the rub. She swallowed and took a long gulp of champagne before saying, "To be honest, I have no idea. At first I thought he'd asked me to work on the Alfa to sweeten me up, so I wouldn't have Jason arrested. But I told him I wouldn't, and he's still hanging around."

"What's wrong with that? He's hot, rich and a nice guy."

She couldn't refute Stella's words. "I keep thinking about Jason. I know he's done rotten things to me, but if he doesn't get help for his addiction, he'll die. I don't know what Jason will think if he finds out I'm... dating... Kade. I know Kade's worried, too. I see through his smiles. Hidden in his eyes is guilt. How can we build a relationship before Jason is well? And will Jason always come between us?"

Stella put down her drink. "Don't get me wrong, I think that's admirable, but Jason being an addict is not your fault and not your responsibility. You can't let him emotionally blackmail either of you. His actions are his alone, and he carries the blame. Only *he* can sort his shit out, and if he ever gets sober, he must know there is no going back after what he's done. How could you ever trust him again?"

Should she tell them about his phone call? Jason wanted her back, but that was still Jason the addict.

A part of her knew what Stella said was right. She owed Jason nothing. But Kade—Kade was his brother. She hated the look of guilt she saw deep in his eyes sometimes when Kade looked at her. She didn't want to cause a rift between brothers.

"Well, nothing has happened between us. And I think that's good until we find Jason. Maybe once this is behind me, Kade and I can see about more.

Kendra raised a glass. "Let's drink to new beginnings. New beginnings for Jason, and for you and Kade."

"I'd rather drink to getting my cabin back," she said dryly.

The next day, Lexie accompanied Kade to his gym. During breakfast, which had been fun, he'd convinced her to come along to watch him practice.

Upon entering the gym, the scents of sweat, leather, and aftershave reached her. Oddly, it was a pleasant combination. Looking around, it surprised her to see a few women present, and then she thought she shouldn't be surprised since boxing and fighting were becoming more popular among females.

Everywhere she looked, people were in motion. Several men were punching heavy bags while a man and woman sparred in one of the boxing rings. Almost all the weight machines were in use and several people were jumping rope. Around the perimeter of the large gym was a running track, on which several people jogged.

Her attention came back to Kade when he lightly rested a hand on her shoulder. "Lexie, this is Calvin Nunez, my good friend and trainer."

A man of Latin descent, who appeared to be in his late forties, smiled at her. Although he was only a few inches taller than Lexie, his black t-shirt with cut-out arms showed off a muscular body, and he seemed to exude power.

"Nice to meet you, Lexie. I didn't know he was seeing anyone." He nudged Kade with an elbow and waggled his eyebrows at her. "I see why he was holding out on me. He didn't want me trying to steal such a beautiful woman away. You're definitely out of his league."

Lexie blushed as she laughed. "Thanks, Calvin. Nice to meet you, too." She didn't know how to respond to his remark about her and Kade seeing each other since they weren't officially dating, so she didn't mention it.

Grinning, Kade said, "I'll go change, Lex. Be back in a few." He pointed at Calvin. "Behave yourself while I'm gone."

Calvin shrugged. "I'll try but no promises."

Kade chuckled and headed for the men's locker room.

"So, how long has this been going on?" Calvin asked.

Lexie fidgeted with her car keys. "Um, well, not long. It's just a casual thing."

Calvin's right eyebrow arched, and he tilted his head a little. "Lexie. Oh, you're Kade's ex-sister-in-law. He's mentioned you a few times. Sorry about the divorce, but between you and me, you're trading up."

Lexie didn't have time to respond because a guy across the room called to Calvin.

"I better get over there before Brant loses his cool, but I'll be back to train Kade," he said before leaving her.

Trying to tamp down her ire over Kade talking about her business with other people, Lexie waited for him to come back. When he did, she pounced. "So, Calvin seems to know a lot about me."

Kade pretended to play with his boxing gloves. "Oh? What did he say?"

Lexie folded her arms. "He knows I'm your ex-sister-in-law, and he said that I'm trading up. Exactly how much *does* he know about me?"

Kade took gauze and tape out of his gym bag that sat on a metal folding chair near them. "Not much more than that. He knows what an ass Jason is, so I'm not surprised he'd say something like that. I told Calvin that I felt bad that he hurt you so much, but I promise that was all I said to him. I didn't air your business, Lexie."

Lexie pursed her lips as she tried to decide whether to believe Kade. His direct gaze convinced her, and the tension in her shoulders ebbed away. "Okay. I believe you." Embarrassment stole through her as she realized how much distrust she harbored towards men. "I'm sorry. I don't mean to be bitchy or suspicious, but I can't seem to help myself."

Sitting down, Kade gave her a half-smile. "I understand, but I hope at some point you'll see that you can trust me."

Lexi appreciated Kade being so nice, but would she ever trust a man again? How could she ever hope to find someone to share her life with if she continued to be suspicious all the time?

"I'm trying, Kade. Please have a little patience with me."

Kade patted the seat next to him and said, "I will. Now, how about helping me get ready?"

Lexie gave him a dubious look but sat next to him. "What do you want me to do?"

"Nothing too hard. I need help to tape my wrists, so it would be great if you'd do it for me since Cal is busy."

Lexie liked a challenge and learning new things, so even

though she was apprehensive, she was also eager for Kade to show her what to do. "Where do I start?

Kade handed her a roll of medical tape. "Have you ever used an Ace bandage on someone?"

Lexie nodded. "I've bandaged Jason's wrists, ankles and knees tons of times over the years."

"Good," Kade said. "Start two inches above my wrist and, keeping the tension on the tape even, come down over my wrist. But don't tape over the bottom part of my palm. Take the tape between my thumb and forefinger and then around my knuckles twice."

Lexie smiled but didn't comment further as she concentrated on the task at hand. She followed Kade's instructions carefully, winding the tape and threading it between each of Kade's fingers. She enjoyed the process, and also the contact with Kade's warm skin. A few times she caught him watching her face instead of her hands and knew that he was thinking about their embrace yesterday.

As she worked, Lexie noticed little scars on Kade's knuckles, most likely from past fights. His hands were large and powerful, and she could only imagine how much pain he could mete out during a match. And how much pleasure if she let him touch her.

His favorite pastime seemed incongruous with his profession and temperament. Of course, Kade was a study in contradiction, so it wasn't all that strange. She liked his nice-guy side very much, but she was curious to see what he was like as a fighter.

"How many fights have been in?" she asked.

"I've lost count," he said. "I started boxing when I was nineteen, which was ten years ago."

"Wow. That long ago, huh?"

"Yeah."

"What got you interested in it?"

"Well, when I was about seventeen, I entered my rebellious

phase and got into some hot water. You know how it is. I stayed out all night, drank, and didn't do my homework," he said.

"You didn't do your homework? I find that hard to believe."

"Why? Because I'm a writer?"

Lexi wasn't sure how to answer without offending Kade. "I guess it's just that you seem sort of scholarly."

Kade laughed. "So, what you're saying is that I seem like a dork or a nerd."

"Not at all. You definitely don't look like any nerd I've ever seen." Lexie ripped off the tape and smoothed down the end. "I just meant that you seem smart and more like the guy who would be good in school instead of a juvenile delinquent."

Kade grasped his taped wrist and squeezed, securing the tape even more and testing Lexie's handiwork. "Well done. Okay, now for the other one."

Lexi was proud that she'd done a good job and set about taping Kade's other hand and wrist with zeal.

Kade watched her for a few moments before continuing his story. "I guess it'll surprise you even more to hear that I dropped out of high school because my grades were terrible, and I didn't want to do an extra year just to graduate. I thought since my parents were rich, I didn't have to do anything with my life. I had a nice trust fund. So you see, I could have ended up just like Jason."

She stopped and looked him in the eye. "But you didn't. That shows the difference between you and Jason."

Kade shook his head. "I met Pastor Sal. He changed my life."

Lexi placed a thick gauze pad over Kade's knuckles and started anchoring it in place. "How did you meet him?"

"I got arrested for underage drinking and got charged with a misdemeanor. I was fined and also had to do community service, which was when I was assigned to help at the mission. Pastor Sal took me under his wing and straightened me out. He convinced me to get my GED and helped me get into community college.

Once all my general-ed classes were out of the way, I transferred to UCLA and got my bachelor's in journalism."

"I'm glad Pastor Sal got through to you," Lexie said.

"Pastor Sal tried to help Jason too. I think Jason tried, but as soon as he got on the racing circuit he became a different man."

Lexie squeezed his hand. "You tried. That's all you can do. Besides, it would've been a shame for the racing community if you hadn't gotten into journalism."

Kade tilted his head a little. "Really? Why?"

"Because you get to the heart of the industry. You don't paint it all as glamor and fame," Lexie replied. "You tell it like it is."

"So, you like my stuff, huh?"

The pride in his voice amused Lexie. "Yeah. I've read a book or too. I don't know much about writing, but I think you have a great voice, or whatever they call it."

"That's exactly what they call it, and thanks. I'm glad you think so."

"I do." She checked her tape job and thought it looked good. "Does that seem okay?"

"It's great. Awesome job. I appreciate the help." He flexed his biceps. "Are you ready to watch Lightning and Thunder in action?"

Lexie rolled her eyes, but inside she was brimming with anticipation. "Yeah, I'm ready."

Standing, Kade said, "As soon as Cal helps me with my gloves, we'll get this show on the road. Be right back."

L exie's heartbeat thudded as if a rock band drummer was performing inside her chest. Kade had been in the ring for fifteen minutes with a man named BJ. The guy was two inches taller than Kade and his face resembled granite. The size difference didn't seem to faze Kade, though. He fought with determination and grit, dodging punches and landing blows.

He'd taken his shirt off, and his torso glistened with sweat. Lexi admired the defined muscles of his chest as they rippled with each movement. Hunger washed over Lexie, and she wanted to run her hands over Kade's slick body. The intensity of her craving startled her, but she didn't shy away from it. Kade wanted her, he wasn't hiding his feelings too well, so why should she deny herself pleasure?

Kade landed a hard blow to BJ's jaw, stunning him. BJ stumbled backwards and shook his head. Lexie let out a little yelp and clapped her hands. Kade flashed her a little smile around his mouth guard but immediately returned his attention to the fight. The bout lasted another fifteen minutes before Calvin declared Kade the winner.

Excited by Kade's win, Lexie jumped up and down a little and cheered as Kade exited the ring. Calvin congratulated him before Kade walked over to Lexie, who handed him a towel sitting on a nearby stand.

"That was amazing," she said. "You were great!"

Kade started wiping sweat from his body, and Lexi was jealous of the towel. The urge to touch him almost overpowering.

"Thanks. I do all right." A cocky look entered Kade's eyes. He noticed the appreciation in her gaze. "I'm glad you enjoyed yourself."

"I did. Thanks for inviting me."

"No problem." A provocative smile curved Kade's lips. "I'm hitting the shower. Care to join me?"

Despite them being in a public place, Lexi was sorely tempted to accept his invitation. "I appreciate the offer," she glanced around at the other men in the gym, "but I don't like an audience when I'm naked."

Kade chuckled. "Okay, but if you change your mind, you know where I'll be."

"Don't hold your breath."

K ade smiled at her sassy retort before heading to the locker room. He started the shower, and stripped out of his boxing shorts. Stepping under the spray, he let the warm water run over him. It would help prevent his muscles from stiffening up after the heavy exertion.

His thoughts turned to Lexie, and he imagined the way her hands would feel on his wet body. That image sent blood racing to his groin, and he started getting hard.

He wanted Lexie more than he had any other woman, but it wasn't just a physical craving. Yes, he wanted to get her into bed, but he also wanted to have a real relationship with her.

Jason's face swam into his head, and he viciously shook it away. This wasn't about Jason. It was about him and Lexie.

It appeared she was letting her defenses down, but he knew it would take time for her to completely trust him.

To keep an erection at bay, Kade mentally reviewed his sparring match, concentrating on that instead of making love with Lexie. He quickly finished his shower, dressed and rejoined her in the gym.

Chapter Twelve

When Lexie arrived at work the next morning, it thrilled her to find that Zip had finished welding the floorboards on the Alfa. Now she could start the paint job. Excitement zinged through her at the prospect. She hurried to the computer workspace to check on the status of her order. According to the email confirmation, her paint had arrived yesterday.

She also called another vendor concerning some minor hoses, and was pleased to find they would arrive later today. If everything came in on time, and the orders were correct, Lexie calculated that she could finish Kade's car by next Monday. It was Wednesday now, which meant she had five days to complete the paint job if she worked through the weekend.

She gave a mental shrug. She'd done that plenty of times, and since she had no plans, it didn't bother her. Plus, detailing jobs didn't seem like work to her. It was an outlet for her artistic passion.

As she finished writing and sending a thank-you email to the paint company, she saw Tom approaching her with a smile on his face. "Well, you seem chipper this morning. You must have gotten some sleep last night," she said.

"Some. A little more than usual lately." He gave her a sly smile. "So, I was driving by Golden Gloves Gym and saw your Jeep there."

Lexie's eyes widened in surprise. "Why were you going by there? It's not on the way to work."

"No, but it *is* on the way to Marcus'. I had to go by his place to get a circular saw I need to finish cutting down some doors at the house. He borrowed it from me two weeks ago," Tom replied.

He'd bought a rundown house a few years ago because of its large lot. Originally, he'd planned to renovate it, but one of his buddies, who was a contractor, had told him he'd be better off to tear it down and build a new one.

Once he and Kendra had gotten married, they'd built a house on the property. It was almost finished, but there were still some things that weren't completed, doors to a few of the rooms being one of them.

He nudged her shoulder. "What gives? Are you guys seeing each other?"

Damn it! Lexie couldn't believe her bad luck. "Please don't tell Kendra. I don't really want anyone to know."

"We never keep secrets."

Lexie could believe that. They had the perfect marriage even after their rocky start. Tom had gotten Kendra pregnant, and he hadn't learned about his son for three years. A huge miscommunication, but it turned out all right in the end. It gave her hope. "Define 'seeing each other.'"

"C'mon, Lex. This is me you're talking to. You don't have to hide anything from me. What's so wrong with you having some attention from a great guy?"

Lexie glanced around to see if anyone was listening. There were usually ears everywhere in the garage. "Let's talk somewhere else."

Tom nodded. "Right. How about the office? Marcus isn't here right now."

"Okay. I don't want him to know anything about this."

Following Tom, Lexie didn't know what she'd tell him once they were alone. She didn't want to talk about it, not yet. How could she explain it to Tom when she didn't understand it herself?

She sat down in a chair by Tom's desk while he closed the office door.

Once seated, Tom asked, "So, what's going on with you and Kade?"

Lexie laughed and made a helpless gesture. "I really don't know."

"Are you guys spending a lot of time together?"

"We had dinner that one night, and breakfast a couple of times, and we went running in the park yesterday."

Tom leaned back in his chair and played with the right sleeve of his overalls. "Okay. Are you just trying to get along with him while we're fixing his car? Or is it his money you have your eyes on? Kendra told me about the cabin."

Lexie shook her head. "It started as a way to see if he knew where Jason was, but it's not like that now. And," she hung her head, "I did consider that it might be a good idea to keep him around just in case I needed the money for the cabin."

"You don't need him to keep your cabin, I'm happy to help. I don't like the idea that you think you're beholden to Kade—you should be free of all Colters if that's what you wish." Silence fell between them, until Tom shifted in his chair and frowned at her. "Are you gonna tell me what it *is* like, or am I supposed to read your mind?"

"I'll admit that when you first told me to work on Kade's car, I thought Kade would be a great backup plan if I couldn't find my money. I knew he would pay his brother's debt if it kept him out of prison."

"Blood is thicker than water. Of course he wants to help his brother."

"He is a good guy." She sat up straight. "I was wrong for

treating Kade like crap just because he's Jason's brother, so I apologized, and he asked me to dinner." Lexie looked away from Tom. "We had a good time. He took me to the mission where he volunteers, and we helped serve dinner to the poor people in the neighborhood."

Tom's forehead furrowed as he leaned forward and rested his elbows on his desk. "He took you to a soup kitchen for your first date?"

The mixture of disbelief and anger on Tom's face was priceless, and Lexie couldn't hold back a laugh.

Tom's expression relaxed into a smile. "Okay, you got me. Ha ha. Where did he really take you?"

"Oh, that's where he really took me. He surprised me and showed me a different side. He said it would help me think about something else besides Jason, and he was right."

Confusion filled Tom's eyes. "So, you ended up enjoying it?"

"Yeah. I thought he was crazy or being condescending, but he's actually very perceptive and knew it would work."

"I see. And you saw him a few times since then."

Lexie rubbed her hands nervously over her thighs. "That's right."

"Okay. What were you doing at his gym this morning?"

"He invited me to watch him box. It was a lot of fun, and he's really good."

Tom picked up a pen and toyed with it. "Do you like him? Like, romantically?"

Their heated embraces rose in Lexie's mind, and warmth rushed through her body. "Uh, yeah… I think I do."

A doubt-filled smile crossed Tom's face. "Are you sure? I mean, doesn't it bother you he's Jason's brother?"

"Yes. It's strange, but I think I deserve a bit of happiness, and Kade is making me happy." Lexie sighed. "Looking back, I see now that I always had to be the responsible one while Jason had fun and got famous. It's like I was his shadow. Towards the end, he treated me more like an inconvenient employee and took it for granted I was willing to accept whatever crumbs of affection he decided to give me."

Tom's right fist tightened around his pen. "I'd like to beat him senseless for the way he treated you."

Lexie would love to see that, but her bitterness was fading. Maybe that was because of Kade's positive opinion of her. It seemed to have taken root and bolstered her self-esteem. Thanks to him, she was seeing that Jason was the unworthy one, not her.

"I appreciate that, but I'm trying to let go of my anger. I don't want him to have that kind of control over me anymore. And he's sick. Addiction is an illness."

"You're always too forgiving, that's why you stayed with him for far too long. Are you sure that jumping into a relationship with Kade is a good idea?"

"I left Jason over nine months ago but really the relationship was over well before that." Lexie's gaze was unflinching. "I've learned my lesson where men are concerned. I'm taking this slow, just testing the waters. I won't get in over my head. I'm happy to wait until Jason signs the divorce papers. But I need Kade's help, and I like who I am when I'm around him."

Tom rested a hand on her forearm. "I'm glad to hear it. I know you're tough and capable, but I'm your friend, and I can't help worrying about you."

Lexie covered his hand and squeezed it. "I know, and I love you for it."

The right side of Tom's mouth lifted in a half-smile. "Right back at ya. Okay. Guess we better get back to it."

Lexie stood. "Agreed. I can't wait to finish painting Kade's car. The undercoat is on but drying. In the meantime, I have some other stuff to do. See ya, boss."

She heard Tom chuckle as she left the office. It felt good to have confided in Tom, and she was glad that he hadn't gotten overly protective like he sometimes did. She appreciated his concern and loyalty, but she had to stand on her own two feet.

As she went to the locker room to change, her thoughts

turned from her best friend to the man she'd left recently at the gym. Kade's charming smile and laugh were fresh in her mind, as were the passionate moments they'd shared before she'd left the gym.

Kade had pulled her into a storage closet in the hallway leading to the backdoor. The fire in his eyes had made her think she was in for some heated kissing, but Kade had surprised her. His assault had been slow, thorough, and devastating. She'd responded in kind, exploring his mouth and winding her arms around his neck.

By the time they'd broken apart, both of them were breathing heavy. Need had hummed through her body and she'd had to dig down deep to find the strength to stop. If she hadn't, she knew they would've had sex in that closet.

She wanted the first time with Kade to be perfect, and she wanted to be single—her divorce complete.

Just thinking about it created an ache within Lexie as she put on her overalls. She closed her locker door and leaned her face against the cold metal for a few moments, attempting to cool her inner fire. Then she took a deep breath and pulled herself together. She had work to do, and standing around thinking about Kade wasn't getting it done.

Lexie shifted her mind into work mode and headed for her mechanics bay.

Chapter Thirteen

The following Monday morning, Kade was driving to Bad Boy Autos just after eight a.m. Anticipation to see his finished car made it hard for him to resist putting the hammer down. Lexie had asked him not to come until they'd finished it because it made her nervous to have someone looking over her shoulder during the process. His trust in Lexie's abilities was complete, and Kade knew that whatever she had come up with would be great.

He pulled into the garage's parking lot and looked at Lexie's bay, but the door was down, so he couldn't see anything. He got out, locked his car, and headed for the office, excitement quickening his steps.

Entering the office, Kade spotted Lexie sitting at Tom's desk. They were looking at Lexie's large sketch pad, no doubt at one of her designs. Her hair, piled on top of her head in a messy bun, exposed her pretty neck. Kade wanted to start at her nape and kiss his way down to her shoulders.

He jumped when someone clapped him on the back. "Looks like someone's here to see his car."

Kade recognized Sully's voice and smiled when he came to

stand beside him. He was about to respond, but Lexie let out an uncharacteristic squeal and rushed over to him.

"Come with me," she commanded, grabbing his hand.

She looked as excited as Kade felt, and he laughed as she pulled him towards the shop door. Tom and Sully followed.

"She gets like this every time she's showing a customer their finished car," Tom remarked.

"She's worse than a kid at Christmas," Sully chimed in.

"Shut up, guys," Lexie tossed over her shoulder.

Kade allowed Lexie to drag him along, enjoying holding her hand. Her eyes glittered with anticipation, and her cheeks flushed. She looked sexy and cute, and Kade couldn't suppress the hunger she created within him.

Arriving at Lexie and Sully's bay, he saw they'd hidden his car from sight under a tarp. He shot a frown at Lexie and gestured at the car. "You're killing me here, and you know it. Take the tarp off."

Lexie and the other mechanics laughed at his cranky order.

She wagged her index finger at him. "Not yet. Close your eyes."

Kade put his hands on his hips. "Really? C'mon."

"Really. Do it. Please?"

The way she pretended to pout made Kade smile, and he shut his eyes. "Okay. They're closed. Now, hurry."

Laughter accompanied the rustling sound of the tarp as they removed it from the car, and the anticipation was almost too much for Kade to bear.

"Okay. You can look now."

Opening his eyes, Kade's gaze took in the sight before him.

What had been a scrap-heap Alfa Romeo Spider past its prime had been transformed into a true work of art. The racing red gleamed like a woman's lips, flush with red lip gloss.

Entranced, Kade followed their progress around to the front of the Alfa. The center of the hood came alive, a garden sprouting and a fountain spraying water so clear and cool, he almost wanted a taste.

He opened the driver's door and looked inside. The cream upholstery smelled like vintage leather when he knew it wasn't old. The burgundy carpet with the walnut dash made the car deserve the name of classic Alfa Romeo Spider.

A collector would pay a fortune for this car, and he hadn't even heard the engine turn over.

Unexpected tears took him by surprise as raw emotion rushed at him. A wall of grief, regret and love crashed down on Kade, the tears burning behind his eyes. He'd bought this heap merely as an excuse to keep Jason's wife from throwing his addicted brother in jail. He'd never expected to love this master-piece—or to feel the way he did about Lexie.

A soft touch on his forearm drew his attention away from the car. He looked down into Lexie's concerned eyes. "Are you okay?"

Kade couldn't speak because of the emotions clogging his throat. Even though he was a writer, for several moments, he couldn't find the words to describe how he felt.

Wiping away another tear, he got himself under control and nodded. "Sorry about that. I wasn't expecting to feel such a connection to—to—a car."

Lexie's eyes brightened with tears of her own. "You like her then?" she said.

"Like? I *love* the car. She's beautiful. Just like you." He didn't care who heard.

Sully cleared his throat while Lexie's face burned bright red.

Kade motioned at the car. "This is amazing. What does the engine sound like?"

Lexie waved him forward. "Hop in."

He lowered himself into the sporty bucket seat and turned the key. The little beauty gave a deep growl as he revved her a bit, but then the engine purred.

His gaze encompassed the others present before settling on Lexie. "The car's phenomenal."

A pleased and relieved smile lit up Lexie's features. "I'm so glad you like it."

Kade wanted to hold her and show her how grateful he was, but that was impossible at the moment. "I don't just like it, I love it." He flashed her a grin. "Now, how about we go for a spin, and you can show me what she can do?"

Lexi's smile widened into a grin and she clapped her hands together once. "Now you're talking! I'll just get my sunglasses."

———

That night, Lexi squeezed the steering wheel of her Jeep until her knuckles turned white. She tried not to panic, but it was difficult. She berated herself for accepting Kade's dinner invitation. He wanted to celebrate the completed restoration of his car. He'd told her to wear something nice because he was taking her to a high-end restaurant.

As soon as the words "sure, that would be great" had come out of Lexie's mouth, anxiety had set in. How could she have been so stupid? Lexie knew the answer to that question. Their test ride had been thrilling. The Alfa had run like a dream, drawing envious gazes as they'd driven through the city and up into the hills along a winding road. The gears had shifted smoothly, with no lurching or shimmying, and the powerful engine had sent them speeding along, climbing the hill with ease.

Driving the car wasn't the only thing that had excited her, though. Kade sitting next to her, laughing and talking, had been just as invigorating. He'd teased her about her driving and then cringed when she'd really put the hammer down. She'd taken pity on him, and pulled over so they could switch.

Although she'd ridden with Kade before, seeing him in command of the powerful car was far different—and arousing.

The skillful way his large hands had handled the wheel and worked the gear stick had conjured images in her mind of those hands on her body. She'd concentrated on the road after that, afraid that he'd see her reaction in her eyes.

They'd arrived back at the garage, and he'd killed the engine but made no move to get out. He'd grinned over at her. "Damn, that was fun. I knew you would do a great job, but it's even better than I'd hoped. Let me take you to dinner to show my appreciation. And I mean to a real restaurant. What do you say?"

Caught up in the moment, Lexie had said, "Sounds great."

"Good. Dress up, because the place I have in mind requires formalwear."

That was when Lexie had regretted accepting his invitation, but she couldn't back out.

Now, she wanted to redo the moment and turn him down, not because she didn't want to go—but because she had nothing suitable to wear and couldn't afford to buy anything.

An idea came to her then, and she asked Google to call Kendra.

"Hi, Lexie. I heard Kade loved his car."

"He did, thanks. It was a dream working on it, but I have a favor to ask."

"Anything."

Lexie mentally crossed her fingers. "Kade asked me out to a fancy dinner tonight, which is great, I think."

"You think? Do you like him?"

Lexie smiled. "I do. Is that crazy since he's Jason's brother?"

"I don't think it is. From what Tom says, he's a good guy. If Tom likes him, that says something. You know how suspicious Tom can be," Kendra replied.

"That's an understatement," Lexie remarked. "He's so different from Jason that most of the time I forget they're brothers. Kade is smart, considerate, and—"

"Hot?" Kendra interjected.

Lexie let out a laugh. "Yeah, he is. Smokin' hot. Watching him box a few days ago was very… stimulating, to say the least. All those delicious, sweaty muscles in action…"

Kendra broke into laughter. "I know exactly what you mean."

Lexie sobered as she remembered the main reason for her call. "So, I'm short on cash, and I have nothing in my closet to wear to a swanky place. Do you have anything I could borrow?"

"Hmm. Let me think," Kendra said. "Yes! I have some things that would work."

Relief loosened the knots in Lexie's stomach. "You're a lifesaver. Can I come over now to pick something? Kade is picking me up at seven."

"Absolutely. We'll make you look drool-worthy."

"Thanks. You're the best."

"I know," came Kendra's cheeky reply.

Lexie chuckled and said goodbye. She ended the call and took the next left. During the fifteen-minute drive, she allowed her excitement about going out with Kade to grow. It had been forever since she'd gone out to dinner with anyone she fancied, and she intended to make the most of every minute.

Kade pulled into the parking lot of Lexie's building and turned the key to cut the engine. It seemed a little odd to be going on a date with Lexie, even though they'd kissed several times. But this felt more official, and he hoped things wouldn't be awkward between them at dinner.

He got out and straightened his suit jacket as he looked at Lexie's building. The pewter-gray structure with white shutters was attractive and seemed to be in good repair. He was glad to see that she lived in an okay neighborhood. Striding to her door, Kade used the silver knocker to announce his arrival and waited.

It had been a long time since Kade had been struck speechless, but when Lexie answered the door, she looked so incredible his brain ground to a halt and blood fled south.

The deep purple spaghetti-strap dress she wore showed off just enough cleavage to tantalize him. It clung to her hips and ended a few inches above her knees. Her long legs, toned yet shapely, were pure femininity. He didn't stare at her long enough to be creepy, but he trailed his gaze up Lexie's body, taking in every luscious inch until he locked eyes with her.

"Stunning."

Her eyes traveled over his gray linen suit and pink shirt and dark gray tie. "Likewise," she said.

Lexie's sexy grin made Kade want to rip off that dress with his teeth.

To break the silent tension, she said, "I'll get my purse."

Kade stepped closer. "We could always order in."

His meaning was clear, but although he could see it tempted her, she resisted. "Oh no. You're not getting off the hook that easy, buddy. I'm not missing out on a fancy meal. Besides, I put too much effort into dressing up to stay home."

"You're right. I want to show you off."

Lexie got her purse and locked up. "Okay. Ready."

Kade offered his arm. Lexie took it and let him lead her to the car. He opened the door and shut it for her once she was seated.

On the way to the restaurant, they chatted about everything but what was important—what the hell were they both doing and where was tonight going.

The fancy eatery, Chez Ramone, intimated Lexie as soon as they got out of the car at the valet station. It had been years since shed been to such a swanky place.

Kade warned the valet dressed in his crisp uniform that there would be dire consequences if anything happened to his car. The young man's eyes had gone wide when he realized he'd get to drive the beautiful sports car, but he hastily assured Kade that he'd take excellent care of the vehicle.

Taking Kade's arm again, Lexie felt proud to be with him as he led her inside. They were shown to their table after only a few moments, where Kade helped seat Lexie. She wasn't used to anyone doing that for her, and it felt a little awkward. Nice, but strange.

She felt like a princess as she looked around. Small crystal chandeliers hung throughout the dining room, and candles were lit on almost all the tables. The lighting was low, and the candle flames created a warm, intimate ambiance. White tablecloths with gold lace overlays covered the tables, and silverware gleamed on their surfaces.

Any moment now, she expected the manager to show up and give her lessons on which silverware to use for each course. That thought prompted her to run a fingertip over a fork lying in front of her. *This* is *the salad fork, right?*

Through her eyelashes, she looked across the table to see if Kade was watching her. To her surprise, he was also studying the table settings. He looked just as perplexed as she was. His left eyebrow arched as he picked up the tiniest fork, which tickled the hell out of her. A giggle slipped out before she could suppress it.

Kade looked over at her with a sheepish grin. "I've never understood why the hell they use so many forks. One is all I need."

"Exactly," Lexie said. "One knife, one spoon, one fork. They do the job just fine. Heck, I'll even use a spork if that's all they have."

As though conjured by magic, a maître d' seemed to materialize by their table. "Good evening, sir, madam. I'm Jared, and it's my pleasure to be your server tonight."

Kade regarded him with a bored, sophisticated expression. "Very good, Jared." He motioned at the silverware. "There are too many forks on here."

Somehow, Lexie held back a snort over his playacting.

Jared's forehead creased. "Too many forks, sir?"

Kade nodded. "Yes. That's what I said. I would prefer that you take away all but the biggest forks for myself and my beautiful dining companion. Or better yet... do you have any sporks?"

Lexie lost it at the shock on Jared's face. A loud peal of laughter escaped her, drawing the eyes of several diners. She didn't give a rip. Kade also laughed, and Jared's mouth curved up in a small, uncertain smile, not sure what the joke was.

She followed Kade's lead when he started gathering up the "extra" silverware. He took hers and handed it all to Jared, who looked like he wanted a crevasse to open in the floor and swallow him up.

His face turned red as Kade patted the metallic bundle now gripped in his hands. "There. That's much better. Thanks."

"Yes, um, you're welcome. I'll just get rid of this and be back in a moment."

They dissolved into quiet laughter as Jared went on his way, neither able to speak for several moments.

Lexie took a tissue out of her purse and dabbed tears from her eyes. "Good thing I wore waterproof mascara, but that would've made it totally worth ruining it."

"I just couldn't resist."

"I'm glad." Lexie rearranged her remaining utensils. "I wonder if he knows what a spork is?"

That set them off again, and they were still laughing when Jared returned. They calmed down as he gave them the wine list and menus. With a stiff smile, he left them to deliberate on their meals and retreated again.

"Wow. Someone's got a big stick up his ass," Lexie commented as she perused the beef selections.

Kade chuckled. "To be fair, he handled our joke fairly well."

Opening her menu again, Lexie studied it. "Right. And whenever Jared gets back, he can recommend something to me."

Jared arrived before Kade could respond and helped her find something to her liking. By the time she chose something, she'd discovered that Jared was actually very nice and a little more down to earth than she'd thought.

Once he'd taken their orders, she laid her napkin over her lap and said, "I think he's warming up to us."

"No, he's warming up to *you*," Kade said.

"Do I detect a bit of green in your eyes?" Lexie teased.

Kade nodded. "More than a little, but I can't blame the guy. You make my temp gauge light up."

Lexie laughed. "Oh, my god. I didn't know you were so tacky."

"It's garage talk. I thought it would put you at ease." Kade waggled his eyebrows. "Just wait. You ain't seen nothin' yet, sweetheart."

Chapter Fourteen

B y the time dessert arrived, their banter had loosened up Jared, and Kade was pleased to see Lexie enjoying the evening.

Lexie ordered the filet mignon, roasted asparagus, and potatoes. She'd devoured her meal with a combination of proper etiquette and ravenous appetite.

Watching her enjoy her food had increased Kade's enjoyment of his own. The way she savored her ginger layer cake with wine-poached pears and cream cheese frosting was erotic. She closed her eyes when she took a bite, slowly drawing her fork from between her lush lips.

Damn. He could almost taste the sweetness of the decadent treat mixed with Lexie's own taste. He wanted to feel her in his arms, and—

Kade put the brakes on those thoughts when his groin tightened. It was hard to control himself around Lexie, but he didn't want to scare her off. So, for now, he settled for watching her and biding his time.

When the last bite of her dessert disappeared, Lexie laid her fork down and regarded him with a contented expression. "That was amazing. I'm about ready to burst."

Kade said, "I'm glad you enjoyed it."

She reached across the table to lay her hand over his. "I enjoyed everything; the food, the ambiance—but most of all, I liked spending time with you."

From experience, Kade knew that alcohol loosened lips and allowed people to say what they truly felt. As he turned his hand over and curled his fingers around hers, Kade suspected that this was the case with Lexie, but he hoped that it was also the truth.

"Same here, honey. I'm so glad you came out with me."

Lexie squeezed his hand. "Me, too. Thanks for showing me such a good time. I don't remember when I've had so much fun."

"I'm glad it was with me."

"So am I."

When Lexie's eyes misted over, Kade knew that it was time to leave before she started crying. He stood up and held his hand out to her. "What do you say we get out of here?"

"Great idea." She took his hand and rose to her feet.

Kade steadied her when she took a shaky step. "Looks like it's time to get you home," he said.

Lexie giggled and held on a little tighter. "I guess so. That wine has a sneaky kick to it."

Kade had only drunk a glass and a half before switching to water. He was glad he'd appointed himself as the designated driver, since Lexie was in no condition to get behind the wheel.

"Whoa, there," he said, putting an arm around her waist.

Lexie's eyes were a little glassy as she smiled up at him. "Thanks. I guess I drank more than I thought."

Kade chuckled as he started guiding her through the dining room, keeping her from bumping into tables along the way. Jared caught up with them, carrying the check portfolio.

Lexie held out a hand to the waiter. "It's been nice meeting you, Jared. I'll come back sometime, and I'll ask for you." She gave his chest a friendly poke. "Because you're the guy I want waiting my table. Not Barney, or Vivian, or Edward, just you."

Where did she come up with those names, Kade wondered?

Jared grinned. "It's been a pleasure, and I look forward to seeing you both again."

Kade took out his wallet and gave Jared a credit card. "Jared, you turned out to be a pretty cool guy." He handed some money to the waiter. "Take this for all the great service tonight."

Jared stared at the hundred Kade held out to him. "Sir, that's too generous."

Lexie snatched it out of Kade's hand, tucked it into Jared's lapel pocket, and gave him a peck on the cheek. "No, it's not. Buy yourself something nice."

Jared turned deep pink and cast a wary glance at Kade. "Thank you, Lexie. I will. I'll be right back with your card."

Kade smiled at the way Jared hurried off. Who could blame him for developing a little crush on Lexie? After all, he'd had one ever since he'd met her. He'd been able to hide it, especially since he made himself scarce a lot once she and Jason had gotten engaged. He'd never cheated on any of his girlfriends, but these past few weeks, he'd learned Lexie was the reason he'd married none of them.

His chest felt like it was caught in a vise grip as that realization hit him. Looking down at the beautiful, slightly intoxicated—wholly intoxicated, woman at his side, the fact that he loved Lexie became as clear as a brand-new pane of glass. Lexie was speaking to him, but he couldn't focus on her words over the timpani-like heartbeats echoing off his rib cage. *I. Love. Lexie.*

It was as simple and as complex as that. He admitted that to himself—welcomed the admission. Just like he sought the truth whenever he was working on a story, he also demanded honesty from himself.

He had to find Jason. He owed his brother the truth, no matter how much it hurt.

Knowing that he was in love with Lexie gave him a tremendous charge, but it also presented a whole host of problems, the first of which was that Lexie wasn't ready to hear that he had such intense feelings for her.

Fuck. Now what do I do? He had no clue how to handle this wonderful, new complication, but for the moment, he knew that he should get Lexie home so she could sleep it off. He was glad when Jared returned with his credit card and receipt. It distracted him from his musings and let them get out of the restaurant.

He kept Lexie upright while they exited the establishment and waited for the car. When the valet drove up, Kade slipped him a fifty and quickly put Lexie in the car. As they drove away, Lexie kept up an amusing recounting of their evening, as though he hadn't been with her and needed a play-by-play.

Kade didn't interrupt her because he was enjoying it, but also because it gave him time to think about what came next.

He cursed under his breath that his team still couldn't find Jason. Trust him to realize he's in love with his brother's wife before their divorce was final.

Just then, Lexie went silent before saying, "Pull over. I think I'm going to be sick."

L exie groaned and leaned her feverish cheek against the cool surface of Kade's car. "Just leave me on the side of the road to die," she croaked.

After puking twice, she was wrung out and felt like fire lived inside her skin. Worse yet, her mind was fuzzy from all the alcohol that was slowly making its way through her system. She was sick and woozy and couldn't quite retain what was happening.

Someone brushed her hair back from her face and lifted it off her neck. A breeze blew across her skin, refreshing her a little. "That feels nice."

She recognized Kade's warm chuckle. "Are you feeling well enough to get going again?"

Any kind of motion made her stomach rebel. "I don't think so."

"You can do it, Lex. It's not far now."

Cracking her eyes open, Lexie tried to bring Kade into focus, but he was still a little blurry no matter how hard she tried. Thoughts of stripping naked and falling into her bed made her reach down deep for the strength to go on.

"Okay. Let's go."

Getting back in the car was easy enough, since she was ready to collapse. When the motor started up, she didn't mind the slight vibration as she lay her head back against the seat. But it wasn't long after the wheels started turning again that her stomach rolled.

As though from far away, she watched Kade reach across her body to roll the window down. Soothing night air flowed into the car and she inhaled it deep into her lungs.

"That's it. Just keep taking slow, deep breaths like that."

With a wan smile, Lexie nodded and followed his advice. She felt better, and her eyes drifted shut. "I don't want to be sick in your lovely new car."

She didn't know how much time had passed before she felt herself being lifted, which roused her. "What's happening?" Opening her eyes, she caught a glimpse of trees and stars, but then all she saw was Kade smiling at her.

"It's okay. I'm just getting you inside."

His strength and kindness were comforting. She lay her head on his shoulder. "All right."

Being in Kade's arms gave her a sense of safety, and she relaxed again. Until another bout of nausea hit her. This time when it kicked in, she was in a strange kitchen, retching into the sink while Kade supported her from behind. Finally, her stomach was empty, and her body calmed down.

While she caught her breath, Lexie looked around a little, but didn't absorb most of it. "Where are we?"

"My place. It was closer, and I figured the sooner we got somewhere stationary, the better. You need a nice, cool shower and to go to bed."

Somewhere in the back of her mind, an alarm bell tried to ring, but Lexie slapped it into silence. Kade wasn't the type of man to take advantage of a drunk woman.

"Okay. Sounds good."

"I'll help you undress, but only down to your underwear. The cold water will wake you up enough for you to finish on your own. I have something you can wear to sleep in."

"Okay."

At that moment, Lexie didn't give a shit if Kade saw her naked. All she wanted was to get a shower and then slip in between some sheets. Where that happened was irrelevant to her.

Kade guided her into a bathroom and turned on a light. She was glad that it wasn't harsh. He unzipped her dress and helped her step out of it. She'd lost her heels somewhere along the way.

She heard the spray of a shower, and then Kade said, "Okay. Here we go."

As she stepped under the water, her body rejoiced at its coolness. It felt like heaven as Lexie stood there. A sigh escaped her as Kade drew her hair away from her face. She lifted her head, tilting her face up to the showerhead to let it run over her face.

She became alert enough to notice Kade's arm around her waist, steadying her.

"Think you can take it from here?"

Looking down, she watched the corded muscles in Kade's forearm flex as he started sliding it away, and was fascinated. "Yeah. I'll be fine."

"You sure?"

Feeling a little stronger, she nodded. "I'm sure."

"All right. I'll go get you something to wear and just put it on the chair in here."

"Okay."

He was gone the next moment, and Lexie leaned against the wall to stay upright. The water eased some remaining nausea and she was loath to move. Maybe she could sleep right there tonight.

The image of herself curling up on the shower floor made her laugh at first, but then it seemed so sad. Tears formed in her eyes, which pissed her off. Suddenly, her bra felt like it was strangling her. Reaching behind her, she fumbled with the hooks and gave up after two attempts.

Trying to take it off like a shirt didn't work either. It clung to her torso like a second skin.

"Kade! Where are you? I can't get this fucking bra off!"

A moment later, she heard him enter the bathroom, and he pulled the shower curtain back. Glancing over at him, she saw that he'd changed out of his suit and now wore only board shorts. Even in her drunken stupor, she thought he was red-hot.

"Hi, handsome."

He grinned, and her heart did a slow flip. "Hi, yourself, beautiful. I want to be clear about this. You're giving me permission to undo your bra, correct?"

"Yes, please."

"Okay. If I do that much, will you be all right on your own?"

"I think so."

He gave a nod and within seconds; she felt the hated garment loosen.

"All right. Holler when you're dressed. I'll make sure you get to the kitchen without falling on your face."

"Such a gentleman," she quipped.

Kade chuckled and withdrew. The shower curtain fell back into place, and she was alone again. Lexie slid the bra from her body and had the presence of mind to drop it in the shower instead of on the bathroom floor. She peeled her panties off, and they joined her bra.

She looked around for soap and saw a bottle of men's body-wash on one of the shelves. Better to smell like a man than like vomit, she reasoned. She squirted some into her palm and just ran it over herself since she didn't have a washcloth or anything. The citrus and pepper scent cleared her head a little and she rinsed.

Stepping out of the shower, she found a fluffy blue towel on the aforementioned chair and dried off. Under the towel lie a pair of pink plaid cotton ladies' boxers and a matching t-shirt. A wave of dizziness hit her when she went to put on the shirt, and she thought she would have to call Kade again, but it subsided and finished dressing on her own.

"Kade? I'm ready."

He appeared before her and put an arm around her shoulders. "Come with me."

"I'd love to." Her eyes widened at her blurted innuendo. "I mean, okay. Sure."

Kade just smiled and took her to an open, airy kitchen. They passed through it and exited through a French door onto a deck. "Have a seat here."

With his help, Lexie sank down onto the cushioned deck chair he'd indicated and leaned back in it.

"I'll be right back with something to settle your stomach."

"Okay." Lexie was perfectly content to sit there, looking up at the starry sky. Blinking lights from a plane crossed overhead, and Lexie briefly wondered who was on it. It was a game that she and her grandmother had played when she'd been little.

"Here you go."

She startled a little at Kade's voice. He stood holding a tall, frosty glass out to her. She took it from him and gave it a wary sniff. "Mmm. Minty."

"It's sweet mint water with a little ginger sprinkled in. You need to rehydrate, hence the water, and the mint and ginger are good for nausea. All natural, and it tastes good."

"You sound like a commercial," she quipped.

"Drink the damn drink, Lex," Kade said, sitting down in the chair next to hers.

Lexie smiled and took an experimental sip. There was a hint of sweetness that kept the mint and ginger from being overpowering. He'd served it over ice, and the combination was incredible. She wanted to guzzle it, but she didn't want to lose all the minty goodness, so she forced herself to sip.

She pointed at the glass. "That is amazing. Like, you could bottle and sell it. You *should* sell it."

He smiled at her, his dark eyes shining. "Nah. They'd just want to mass produce it and pump it full of preservatives and chemicals if I ever sold the recipe."

"That's probably true." Lexie took another sip and returned her gaze to the stars.

"Penny for your thoughts."

"My grandmother used to say that. I don't know why, but she popped into my head when I sat down here."

"Didn't she live in the Midwest? I think I heard you mention her a couple of times."

"Good memory. Idaho. Her and Gramps were typical farmers. Salt-of-the-earth people and all that."

"What exactly brought her to mind?"

"The plane overhead. We'd lay out in the yard on warm nights, just talking. She'd tell me stories about when she was young, and when we saw a plane, we'd make up stories about the people onboard. Maybe there was a businessman heading back home to New York from another country. Or maybe a movie star who was going to LA for a premier. Things like that."

"That sounds like fun, and your gram sounds like a cool lady."

Lexie took a sip of her drink and smiled. "She was. I miss her a lot. She died when I was seven, and then life took a bit of a dive."

"You must tell me about it one day, but you need sleep now."

A huge yawn gripped Lexie and her eyelids felt like five-pound bags of sand were sitting on them. Holding up her head suddenly seemed almost impossible. "I think it's time for me to turn in." Her words sounded faint even to herself. She felt the glass being lifted out of her hand, and then she faded into oblivion.

Chapter Fifteen

Voyeurism wasn't Kade's thing, but the sight of Lexie mesmerized him. She slept in his small guest bedroom in his guesthouse. The only other furniture besides the full-size bed was a nightstand, chest of drawers, and a plant stand by a large window. Sunlight poured through it, illuminating the beautiful woman slumbering mere yards from his own bedroom.

Her long hair was wild from her tossing and turning, and it looked like she'd been sweating, judging by the way a large lock was sticking to her forehead. The rest of it resembled a rat's nest, and she was pale with dark smudges beneath her eyes. A light snore emanated from between her slack lips.

A smile curved his mouth before he took a sip of his coffee as he thought even all that hangover-ugly couldn't hide the fact that Lexie was sexy as hell. Her long, bare limbs tempted him to run his hands along them, and he wanted to tug the top sheet from around her body and feast his eyes on her naked form.

His eyes moved over to the dresser where her borrowed PJs had wound up in a wad on the floor next to it. He'd heard her up once during the night, but when he'd gone to check on her, she'd been back in bed. Apparently, she'd been too hot, and had remedied the problem.

Consulting his watch, Kade decided to wake her, since it was almost ten a.m. She would freak out about losing almost a half day's work and missing even more would only drive her crazier. So even though he'd rather stand there gawking some more, he moved away from the door and turned his back.

"Lexie," he called. "Time to get up."

Nothing.

"Lex, time to get up!"

Barely audible mumbling met his ears.

"C'mon. Time to rise and shine. Tom was pretty pissed when I told him you would be late today. He said you guys got an important job in."

"Kade! Why didn't you wake me! Oh, my God. I could kill you!"

Kade almost dropped his coffee mug when she blew by him without a stitch of clothes on. He looked at the bed and then back at the finest female ass he'd ever seen as she streaked to the bathroom.

She disappeared inside and slammed the door shut. A moment later, he heard the shower turn on and she poked her head back out the door. "Do you have more clothes? Something I can wear to the shop? My overalls are in my locker. I'll just change there like I usually do."

Kade stepped a little closer, not even remotely ashamed that he wanted to see more of her. It seemed like the body heat she'd shed during the night had transferred to him. "Um, yeah. I think I do."

"Great. And do you have an extra toothbrush? Oh, and can you get me a rubber band?" She gestured at his head. "It's not like you'd have a hair scrunchie lying around for any reason."

Kade arched an eyebrow. "I'll choose not to be offended by that remark, or the way you're ordering me around. It's just the hangover talking."

She dragged her frizzy hair back from her face. "Hangover? I don't get hangovers. I'm drunk as hell the night of, but the next morning, I'm raring to go as soon as my eyes pop open. Okay, enough chitchat, sexy. Rubber band. Clothes. Toothbrush?"

That she'd just called him sexy only half mollified him. "There's a toothbrush in the medicine chest, but there's no rush."

She rolled her eyes. "Hello? Yes, there is. You just told me that there's a big job at work, remember?"

He grinned and moved closer still, but she stood behind the door enough to hide everything except a bare shoulder and her arm. "Oh, that. I just told you that to get you awake. There's no job. Tom said you should treat yourself to a paid day off since you worked all weekend on my car. Said you earned it."

The satisfaction her surprised reaction brought him made Kade laugh. Anger flashed in her eyes and she slammed the bathroom door, making him laugh even harder.

"Just you wait, Kade! Just you wait."

Her yelled threat amused him, as he went to fulfill her demands. He got a rubber band from a kitchen drawer and more clothes from the chest of drawers in the spare room. On his way to the bathroom to put the items on the chair inside, he changed his mind and detoured to his living room.

He set the clothes on the couch and went to the kitchen, all part of the bungalow's open floor plan design, to get another cup of coffee. After a few minutes, the shower turned off.

"Kade? How are we coming on those clothes?"

"Great. I got them all ready for you."

"Where?"

"Out here."

"What? Why out there? And why are there no towels?"

"They're dirty."

"You only have two towels?"

"No. There are some in the spare room."

"Oh. Can you get me one?"

Kade set his coffee mug on the counter and opened the fridge. "I could. If I wanted to."

Quiet met his words. "Is this payback for last night? I'm sorry I got drunk, okay? I know it ruined the celebration, but in my defense..."

Kade laughed silently as she laid out all the reasons he shouldn't be pissed at her for getting wasted. She was pretty creative with her excuses, which wasn't surprising, given her artistic mind.

"...so cut me some slack and don't be a wuss about it, okay?"

"Okay."

"Now, may I *please* have a towel?"

"I'll think about it."

"Fine! I'll get it my damn self!"

The bathroom door flew open, and Lexie shuffled out, wearing—

No, he had to be imagining it. Wasn't he?

Moving closer, he saw that his eyes weren't deceiving him. Lexie stood glaring at him as she wore a tight dress-like garment made from tropical-theme-printed paper towels. Her hair was damp, but not dripping wet, she'd used some to dry her hair, too.

It was literally the funniest damn thing Kade had ever seen, and he erupted in laughter. He couldn't hear her over it when she started bitching at him. She gave up after a moment and turned away, starting to shuffle towards the spare room. He went to his knees at the sight of her inching along, trying to keep the paper towels from splitting as she moved.

Even through his amusement, Kade wished that the improvised dress would do just that. The paper towels had molded perfectly to her sweet backside and hot blood shot to his groin. He'd never look at Bounty products the same way again. They truly were the quicker picker-upper, judging by how fast his cock had hardened. Struggling to get ahold of himself, Kade wondered how anything could be so hysterical and so erotic at the same time.

Lexie made it to the doorway of the spare room and stopped, leaning against the doorframe. As his laughter started subsiding, he saw Lexie's shoulders shake and a loud giggle escape her.

"This isn't funny!" Her voice quivered though.

Kade got to his feet and approached her. "Yes, it is. This is one hell of a fashion statement."

Lexie bent over as a shout of laughter burst from her, and the "skirt" of her unorthodox outfit ripped up the back. She spun around, pressing her back to the wall as she shook from the force of her mirth.

Seeing her laugh and smile made Kade wish he could make that a daily occurrence in her life. While he'd been writing last night to keep his mind off his desire for Lexie, he'd concluded that his feelings for her had been stronger than he'd suspected. During the time she'd been married to Jason, he'd kept them hidden, even from himself, it seemed. It was the only explanation he had for his rapid acceleration of falling in love with her the past few weeks; he'd already been there.

And so now, he found it even more difficult to not let the words he longed to say spill forth. Biting them back, Kade gathered up the clothes he'd gotten and gave them to her.

"Get these on and I'll make some breakfast." He gave her a slow once-over before bending down to kiss her cheek. Ignoring the way his blood heated, he smiled, turned around, and headed for the kitchen.

L exie sobered as he walked away. His blue tank top showed off his muscular arms and shoulders, and his ass looked incredible in the denim cargo shorts he wore. He was everything she could want in a man. Respectful, funny, considerate, and so hot that she sometimes felt like she was melting when he was near. It had taken every ounce of strength to stay out of his bed.

But what was stopping her from being with him? Her marriage was over even if papers weren't signed, and he was single and unattached. They wanted each other, so what kept holding her back? Hugging the clothes to her chest, Lexie wrestled with indecision. It had been so long since she'd made love that she was afraid she'd forgotten how.

Doubtful. It's just like riding a bike. You can do this. You want to do this. Need to do this. You deserve some happiness. Lexie took courage from her inner voice and decided that she sure as hell had lived with sorrow and despair for far too long. It was time to take her life back—truly back—and allowing herself to be with a man she cared about was a gigantic step in that process. The dark days of mourning were over. Letting Jason make her feel guilty was a waste of her life, and she'd wasted too much on him already. You couldn't change the past, but you could try to create a future you deserved.

It was a new day, and the sun was shining. Lexie let herself bask in its warm glow. A smile started and continued to grow as a sense of well-being she hadn't experienced in what seemed like forever filled her.

Her decision made, she dropped the clothes to the floor as an idea occurred to her. "Kade? Can you come help me?"

"Be right there."

Pots and pans rattled in the kitchen for a moment, and then Kade came walking through the living room. "What's up?"

Trepidation gnawed at Lexie, but she refused to chicken out. Shooting him a flirtatious look, she said, "I was wondering if you'd like to help me out of this?"

Kade's eyebrows shot up, but his eyes narrowed in suspicion seconds later. "Lexie, what are you doing?"

She took hold of the towels wrapped around her breasts and ripped them a bit.

Kade took two steps towards her, but his expression remained wary.

Holding his gaze, Lexie tore it further, exposing more cleavage, and Kade's nostrils flared. His small but telling reaction made her feel powerful and beautiful, and she didn't want the heady experience to end.

"Are you sure you're not still drunk?"

Kade's question made Lexie laugh. "I'm sure. I know you want me, Kade, and you know that I want you, too. I've just been stuck in my head, and I let the fact that you're Jason's brother get in the way. But not anymore."

Coming to stand before her, Kade ran his knuckles down her cheek. "I'm glad you see that I'm nothing like him. I love my brother, but he's a troubled soul. I'd never disrespect you or hurt you like that, Lex."

Lexie fought back the tears that threatened and took his hand. She kissed his palm and rested it against her chest. "I know. I also know that you're incredibly sexy, and that I want to be with you."

Her heart started racing as she slid his hand down to the torn place in the paper towels. She smiled up at him, meeting his questioning gaze with a slight nod.

Instead of ripping the towels off her, he slid an arm around her waist and pulled her against his body. She rose on tiptoe as he brought his mouth down on hers, winding her arms around his neck and pressing closer yet.

She parted her lips and whimpered in approval when his tongue slowly invaded her mouth. He tasted of coffee and peppermint, and she was suddenly ravenous for him. Opening her mouth wider, she deepened the kiss until they were almost devouring one another. She let out a little squeal when he lifted her off her feet and started walking.

The feel of his strong arms around her and his warm, sensual mouth on hers kept Lexie from caring about where he was taking her. It didn't matter as long as he didn't stop. And he didn't until he set her back down. Her chest rose and fell rapidly from her excitement, and she ached in places she hadn't in so long.

"God, I want you, Lexie." His eyes smoldered with dark fire as he cupped her face. "I have for so long."

Lexie shook her head. "I can't believe you said nothing."

"I'm a lot of things, but a home-wrecker isn't one of them," Kade said. "I'd have never come between you and—"

Lexie put a hand over his mouth. "Don't say it. I don't want to think about anything but you and me right now. Okay?"

Kade nodded and she drew her hand away. With a wicked grin, he hooked an index finger at the bottom of the tear in her paper dress. "Same here, but there's something else you should know before we go any further."

She ran her hand over his forearm. "Oh, and what's that?"

"I love you, Lexie."

Her lips parted on a gasp and her eyes went wide. "You what?"

"You heard me. I don't expect to hear it back, so don't feel pressured. I understand that you don't feel the same way, but I just thought it was time you knew how serious I am about you."

Tears welled in Lexie's eyes and she shook her head a little. "I don't know what to say. I'm not ready for that." She squeezed her eyes shut, and a tear fell from her right eye, rolling down her cheek. "I never expected… I just thought… oh, damn it! Why the fuck does this shit keep happening to me?"

Kade laughed, his eyes shining. "That's the oddest reaction I've ever heard when told that someone loves them."

Relieved that he wasn't angry because she couldn't return his feelings, Lexie smiled and brushed away her tears. "You just completely blew my mind. I think I'm shell-shocked or something."

Kade pulled her into his embrace. "Sorry about that, but I just couldn't wait any longer to tell you. I've wanted to for a little while, but it worried me you'd think I was moving too fast. I know you're not on the same page as me, but that's okay. I don't mind."

The intense light in his eyes made her feel like he was looking into her soul. She tried to think of something to say, but nothing came to her. Lexie wished she could be as brave as him. He'd lain himself bare to her, made himself vulnerable in one of the most meaningful ways possible.

"I love you, and if you can't accept that, there's the door."

The intense light in his eyes made her feel like he was looking into her soul, and she knew she had to decide. Could she, Lexie wondered? Was it possible for her to continue a relationship with Kade when she didn't reciprocate his feelings? Meeting his gaze, she felt her heart take a step closer to the edge and accepted his terms.

Her mind made up, Lexie ran her hands over his shoulders, loving the firm muscles under her palms. "I'm not going anywhere."

His sexy grin flashed. "Glad to hear it. Now, I think it's time for me to assist you like you asked me to. I want to see that delectable little body, run my hands all over you, and taste you—everywhere."

Lexie felt weak at just the thought of it, and she almost yelled at Kade to hurry. He put pressure on the towels, and they gave way, no match for his strength. Her nipples tightened as his knuckle skimmed down her torso. He kept going until he reached the point just above her mound. His gaze collided with hers, and again he lifted a questioning eyebrow. She couldn't say why, but she found his eyebrows fascinating. Maybe it was because they added to his expressive eyes, or maybe it was the way they enhanced their beauty.

She nodded her assent and then gasped when he rent the paper towels the rest of the way. They fell to the floor with only a whisper of sound, and Lexie felt a little vulnerable as she stood naked before Kade.

"Holy shit, Lex."

It amazed Lexie that this man who'd written a gazillion words in his lifetime could still say so much with so few. His gaze raked over her, traveling upwards until he reached her eyes.

"You're even hotter than I ever imagined you'd be." He wrapped one arm around her and slid his other hand down her side and around to squeeze her butt cheek. "I've never seen a finer ass. It used to drive me crazy whenever you wore a bikini."

Lexie giggled as he spun her around, and she realized they were in Kade's room. It was bright and airy with large windows. Sheer curtains provided privacy but allowed plenty of light and fresh air into the room.

He pressed against her from behind, still exploring her rear end as he urged her towards his queen-size bed. As soon as her knees touched it, he ran his hands up her to cup her breasts. Lexie's head fell back against his shoulder as he gently kneaded them. She couldn't stand still when he started grazing his fingers over her taut nipples.

Hot need pooled between her thighs as he teased and caressed them. He kissed her shoulder and she shivered at the contact. She pressed her hands over his, inviting him to squeeze a little harder.

"You feel so good in my hands," he murmured in her ear as he complied with her unspoken request. "Not too big, not too small, just perfect."

Lexie smiled. "Sounds like Goldilocks and the Three Bears."

"Well, the guy who wrote that sure knew what he was talking about."

Kade bit her earlobe, and Lexie almost went to her knees as a jolt of pleasure shot straight to her core. "Oh god," she moaned. He sucked on it, and Lexie thought she would lose her mind with excitement. She grabbed one of his hands and drew it down to the juncture between her thighs.

Chapter Sixteen

Lexie's assertiveness made it hard not to throw her on the bed and drill her into the mattress, but Kade wanted this to be an amazing experience for both of them. Especially since he was sure she hadn't been with a guy in quite a while. Even though she hadn't said so, it made sense to him. She'd been going through too much hell to think about hooking up with some random dude.

He didn't want to be a random anything to Lexie. He wanted to be everything to her, but the most important thing was bringing her maximum pleasure. This was a huge step forward for her, for them both, and he refused to screw it up by rushing things.

So, even as he cupped her pretty little shaved mound, he did his best to ignore his rock-hard dick and concentrate on her. He slid a finger between her slick folds as he continued paying attention to her ear and found her clitoris. Her feminine cry had him gritting his teeth as he curbed his reaction.

Kade drew gentle circles around the swollen nub but didn't give her exactly what she sought, because he wanted to see her face the first time he made her come. She pressed her hips forward, seeking release, but Kade withdrew his hand.

Her groan of frustration as she turned to face him made him chuckle.

"Why did you do that?" Her eyes flashed fire at him. "I was almost there."

"Oh, I know you were, but I want to do something you'll enjoy even more."

She poked his chest. "It better make my eyes roll back in my head. Got it?"

"Got it."

He took her hand and kissed it, then playfully shoved her back on the bed. Her laughter as she bounced made Kade glad that he'd opted for humor instead of being too serious. Lexie was most comfortable when she was having a good time, so he would give her fun, sensual, mind-blowing sex.

He stripped off his tank top and started undoing his jeans, but Lexie sat up on the edge of the bed and batted his hands away.

"It's my turn to get you naked."

"By all means, go right ahead."

His breathing sped up as she pulled down his zipper and tugged his shorts down until they fell to the floor. His cock strained against his boxer briefs, jumping a little as his heated blood continued to flow like molten lava.

He kicked his shorts to the side as she began stroking his penis through his underwear. From his viewpoint, her eyelashes looked like tiny dark fans as she gazed at him. Her breasts rose and fell with her breathing, blocking his view of her sex. He didn't know why, but it was one of the most alluring things he'd experienced. *Everything about Lexie is alluring and beautiful.* And it was.

With a seductive glance up at him, she took down his underwear, exposing his pulsing member. From her growing smile, he assumed that she liked what she saw. His underwear followed his shorts, and he got rid of them.

One of Kade's biggest turn-ons was seeing a woman enjoy

herself with him, but Lexie mattered so much to him, he was a little nervous; something he wasn't used to when it came to sex. He'd left behind that kind of insecurity when he'd been much younger—or so he'd thought.

Her smile stayed in place as she closed her fingers around his shaft, but he felt a light tremble in her hand as she started exploring him. It wasn't surprising that she'd be a little anxious and knowing that strengthened his resolve to take it slow.

"I'm on birth control."

Her sudden statement cut into his thoughts, and he didn't know what to say at first because he hadn't even thought about that. He'd been so focused on her it hadn't occurred to him to ask. A first for him. "Good to know. I always use protection."

"Good to know," she parroted with an impish smile as she tightened her grip around him a little and started stroking.

Along with the pleasurable sensations she was creating, Kade enjoyed watching her hand move. It was strong, yet feminine and pretty. She'd painted her short nails a dark red that complimented her light tan.

The confident way she handled him showed that she was enjoying herself, and he didn't want to stop her. With her other hand, she caressed his ball sac, hefting its weight and massaging it. When she started running her thumb in circles on the underside of the head of his cock, he almost came undone.

Cupping a hand around the back of her head, he leaned down, capturing her mouth. She opened for him, meeting his tongue and drawing it inside. He answered her demand and started laying her back on the bed. The action broke her hold on him, giving him a chance to slow things down.

Kade wanted to make this last as long as possible. Lexie deserved more than just a quick lay. He wanted to make her feel special, to show her how much he cared for her.

Hooking an arm around her waist, he lifted and moved her up farther in the bed. She laughed and looped her arms around his neck, pulling him down to press her mouth to his again. The insistent way she kissed him with those sweet lips set Kade on fire.

His penis brushed against her stomach, and the urge to join their bodies was almost too strong to resist. However, a warning bell went off in Kade's mind. He broke the kiss and smiled at Lexie before leaning down to kiss her neck. Her shiver made him smile again as he trailed his tongue down to her left breast. He took the peak in his mouth and created gentle suction.

Lexie's hips rose off the bed, and she gripped his biceps. He teased her other nipple and sucked harder. Lexie dug her nails into his flesh, and her pelvis started undulating. It was time to give her at least a little of what she craved.

Leaving her breasts, he pressed a series of kisses down her stomach to her mound.

She parted her legs, treating him to a view of her. Her pink folds glistened from her excitement and he loved knowing that he affected her so much. He guided her legs open farther and moved lower.

L exie felt like she was lying in front of a raging fire. She ached for release and communicated that to him by her urgent movements. The closer he came to her center, the more she needed him.

When Kade brushed his lips against her, Lexie moaned in anticipation. His tongue slid lower and the first soft glide of it against her clitoris sent an electric current through her body. Her back arched and she ran a hand over Kade's head.

She liked the warm smoothness and thought about how equally smooth and soft and yet hard his cock was. He delved his tongue farther between her folds and swept it upwards, where he focused on the sensitive, swollen nub for a few moments.

Then he opened his mouth wide and covered her with it,

sliding his tongue up and down her. Lexie moaned and came up on her elbows. Those fabulous deep brown eyes of his met hers, and she couldn't look away as she watched him pleasure her.

Kade withdrew and moved up to her clit, flicking across it with light, rapid strokes that had Lindsey quivering in no time. He knew just where her most sensitive nerve endings were and concentrated on them. Her mouth opened and her forehead puckered as she balled the sheet in her hands.

Holding in little whimpers while Kade stroked her was impossible. She was past the point of coherent thought now. Every nerve ending was alive as sheer blissful sensation coursed through her body. Her breathing was shallow and fast as she climbed toward the pinnacle of passion.

A fine trembling overtook her as she neared the summit. "Don't stop. Please don't stop." She didn't mind begging, too desperate to care about sounding needy.

Kade didn't respond, but she knew he'd heard her because he sped up just a hair. It was exactly what she needed.

The first pulse of release made her moan and clutch Kade's shoulders. What began as small, soft waves soon grew, sweeping Lexie along in a swift current that brought her to a shuddering climax.

She seemed to hang there, suspended in ecstasy so intense that it stole her breath. When her lungs started working again, she let out a cry of joy over the last sharp spasm before the sensations began ebbing away.

Her hands flopped onto the mattress, and she looked down at Kade. His mouth left her sex to trail kisses down the insides of each of her thighs before lifting his gaze to hers. He lifted a questioning eyebrow that made her smile, then giggle. It grew into a full belly laugh that she was helpless to fight. His silent inquiry as to how it had been for her was amusing enough, but the happiness he'd brought her compounded her mirth, setting off a laughing fit.

He grinned as he pushed off the bed. His stiff cock bounced a little as he moved to a nightstand. "That good, huh?"

Another jag hit her, and she snorted as tears trickled from her eyes. The only response she could manage at the moment was vigorous nodding. Even if she hadn't been laughing, she really had no words for how amazing he'd made her feel. Her laughter began abating as she watched Kade get a condom out of a drawer and tear the package open with his teeth.

He tossed the package in a little waste can and started rolling the condom down his thick length. The graceful way his fingers moved excited her almost as much as the rest of his delicious body did. His forearm muscles flexed a little as he finished with the condom and stepped over to the bed.

Instead of crawling in right away, he stood, his smoldering eyes moving with infinite slowness over her. Her body came alive everywhere his gaze touched.

"I swear you're the most fuckable woman I've ever seen."

His statement might sound crude and blunt to some women, but the awe in his voice made it as romantic to Lexie as wordy flattery was to other females. She didn't need all that shit. She wanted someone genuine and honest, and Kade was the real deal.

Tossing him a challenging grin, she said, "Then why don't you get over here and do it?"

Kade hardened even more as his gaze traveled over Lexie. Although toned and lithe from all the manual labor she did, she was also womanly and exciting. Her intoxicating taste was still on his tongue and he planned to sample her many times. But he wanted to drive her crazy before completely satisfying her in every way.

He kneeled on the bed and crawled up between her legs, kissing her pretty feet, calves and knees as he went. Reaching her mound, he kissed it and inhaled deeply. He liked the scent of his shower soap, but on Lexie it was the sexiest damn thing he'd ever smelled.

Lexie giggled as Kade dragged her down where he wanted her. She spread her legs wide and gasped when he teased her clitoris with his cock, slowly stroking forward and back before pushing forward again. From the way her nostrils flared as she bit her bottom lip, Kade could tell that his lazy pace was driving her crazy, and he ached to be inside her.

Leaning over her, he claimed her mouth, thrusting his tongue inside just as he found her entrance and gradually sank into her. She moaned into his mouth and grasped his hips, urging him on until he was completely immersed inside her warm sheath. He lay down on Lexie, giving her his weight as they continued to kiss.

He drew back and thrust into her faster this time, burying his cock deep inside. Lexie arched her back and moaned as he began moving his hips. He'd intended to take things slow, to prolong the experience for both of them, but Lexie excited him so much that he wasn't sure he'd be successful.

Judging by the way she moved with him and the small sounds she made every time he drove home, she didn't want to wait. Her wild need for him ratcheted up his own for her. He stroked long, fast, and hard, loving the way her breasts bounced with the force of his thrusts.

"Kade! I can't wait," Lexie called out.

Her flushed cheeks and the way she matched his movements made Kade abandon any thoughts of making it last. But he was damned if he'd give in before he satisfied her.

"Don't, baby. Come for me. I want to make you feel so good. Enjoy yourself, honey."

Her eyes had grown darker, glittering as she met his gaze for several moments before her head fell back. She clutched his back, emitting throaty moans that rose in pitch and volume. A scream erupted from her just as he felt her contract around his shaft.

Kade was rapidly nearing the threshold, and soon there would be no going back. He concentrated on Lexie, tuning out his body's need for completion as he watched and felt intense pleasure surge through the woman he loved.

———

L exie went lax as her powerful release faded. Her breath rasped in her chest, and her heart raced. She yelped in pleasant surprise when Kade shifted position, igniting her desire again. Opening her eyes, the sheer masculine beauty of the man instantly captivated her. Gripping her hips with his large, strong hands. She wanted to feel his hard body move against her and come with him.

She lifted her arms to him, silently inviting him closer. He covered her, kissing her deeply as he pumped in and out. She reveled in his weight, loving the way his back flexed against her palms with each movement. Tension built rapidly for both of them, and a fine sheen of sweat broke out over their bodies.

His eyes practically glowed as they locked gazes. With a feminine growl, Lexie hooked a hand around his neck and brought him down until they touched foreheads.

"I want to watch you, Kade," she said, her voice husky. "I want to see you come with me."

His response to her fierce declaration took her by complete surprise. Kade reared up and hooked his arms under her legs. The defined muscles of his biceps stood out even more. She caught sight of his tattoos. Thunder and Lightning, and she thought them aptly named because he was sweeping her along in a storm of sensation.

His chest and stomach muscles rippled every time he drove into her, and his breath came in ragged pants. Lexie grabbed the headboard and held on as Kade took her on the ride of her life.

Loud whimpers rose from her throat as yet another shattering climax gripped her.

Even as his features tightened, and his shoulders tensed, Kade never looked away from her. A low, guttural growl rumbled in his chest and his big body vibrated, but he held her gaze, and she'd seen nothing so hot in her entire life.

She reached a bliss-filled high just as Kade filled her to the hilt and froze above her. His nostrils flared and his grip on her legs became just shy of painful. A long growl of ecstasy rose from his throat and faded away. "Oh, shit, Lex. Damn, baby!" he moaned before melding his mouth to hers.

Lexie kissed him back just as fiercely, filled with happiness that she'd made him feel so good after all the pleasure he'd brought her. When his body went slack, she pulled him down on top of her. Their hearts thundered together as the tempest calmed.

Caressing Kade's back, she kissed his shoulder and fought back sudden tears. It shocked her to realize that they were happy tears. That had never happened to her before. What they had just shared was beautiful, and even though it scared her, Lexie accepted it and decided to just enjoy.

After a few moments, Kade lifted off her, kissing her before slowly moving away. He cupped her face and smiled at her as he stroked her cheek with his thumb. "I'll be right back. Don't go anywhere."

She laughed and relaxed against the mattress, arms spread wide. "No worries there."

Kade laughed with her and then left the room, headed towards the bathroom, and she sat up, enjoying watching his tight ass as he went before flopping back down. She drifted in a pleasant haze, sated and so relaxed that she felt boneless.

Kade returned and sat on the bed as he handed a glass to her. "Here. I thought you might be thirsty."

Lexie suddenly realized that her mouth and throat were devoid of moisture and took the glass from him. She smelled mint and smiled before taking a huge gulp. It was cool and refreshing after all the heavy breathing she'd done.

When the last drop of the delicious, sweet beverage slid down her throat, she handed the glass back to Kade to sit on the nightstand. Then he made her scoot over and slid into bed beside her. He pulled the sheet over them and gathered her close.

"I think we need a nap after that," he said, brushing a kiss against her temple.

Lexie smiled as she settled against his chest. "That sounds like a great idea." Exhaustion took hold of her as she closed her eyes. The sound of Kade's heartbeat under her ear soon lulled her into a contented slumber.

Chapter Seventeen

Thunder woke Lexie. She blinked and looked around as lightning flashed. Orienting herself, she lifted her head from the pillow and sat up. She felt deliciously relaxed in a way she hadn't in a long time. The incredible experience with Kade came back to her and she smiled. He'd been alternately gentle and fierce, almost turning her inside out.

Turning around, she saw Kade's side of the bed was empty and wondered where he was. She rose and then stopped. What happened now?

Blowing out a breath, she opened one of Kade's drawers and found a t-shirt. She smiled as she slipped on an LA Dodgers shirt. She'd have to harass him about his team, even though she didn't follow baseball.

Leaving the bedroom, she followed the sound of music. It was coming from the direction of the deck. Why was Kade outside in the rain? Drawing closer, she recognized Elvis' "Blue Suede Shoes" and smiled at hearing the golden oldie. Glancing at the kitchen clock, she saw that it was almost three o'clock. It wasn't surprising that she'd slept so long after all the pleasant exertion she'd shared with Kade.

As she walked towards the deck, she noticed the slight

burning sensation along the inside of her upper thighs from Kade's beard. Memories of the languid way he'd pleasured her made her tingle. She'd like a repeat of that.

Stepping out onto the deck, she saw that it was wet, but that the clouds were moving off. The section of deck nearest to the house was almost dry, thanks to the huge awning overhead. She caught the savory scent of meat and forgot about the weather.

Kade stood at a grill, tending to some fantastic-smelling food. He was shirtless and his back muscles flexed as he moved. She had a sudden urge to bite him and run her hands over his powerful body.

He must've heard her because he turned and smiled. "Hi, sleepyhead."

"Hi. How long have you been up?"

She reached his side and he bent down to plant a firm kiss on her lips.

"About an hour. How do you feel?"

The concern in his eyes was sweet and touching.

"Wonderful."

His smile widened and her heartbeat went a little erratic. "Ditto. I see you found something to wear."

She smirked. "I just grabbed the first thing I found. Your taste in baseball teams sucks."

He pointed his spatula at her. "Don't knock the Dodgers."

Chuckling at his response, she motioned at the grill. "What's under that lid?"

"Burgers. I figured you'd be hungry. I know I worked up an appetite."

Lexie fought back a blush. "Yeah, I'm starving."

"Well, it won't be long until they're ready. I'll put the fries on in a few minutes."

Lexie's mouth watered even more. "Homemade French fries?"

Kade nodded. "I do them in an air fryer. They taste awesome and they're a lot healthier. No oil or grease."

"Are you a healthy food nut?" she teased.

"Somewhat, I guess. I watch my diet because of training."

"But you eat burgers."

Kade arched an eyebrow. "Ninety percent lean Angus beef and low-fat organic cheddar cheese."

Lexie wrinkled her nose. "You can keep the cheese. Organic stuff tastes like shit."

Kade lifted a piece of aluminum foil off a plate. Several slices of cheese lay on it. "Try some."

Lexie gave him a dubious look but tore off a corner of one piece. She put it in her mouth and groaned. It wasn't as tasty as regular cheese, but it wasn't gross. "Not bad."

"Told you."

Lexie nudged him with an elbow. "No need to be so cocky."

He just shrugged and lifted the grill lid. Four burgers sizzled on the top rack. The intoxicating smell of charcoal and beef hit her. "When are they going to be done?" She couldn't wait to sink her teeth into one.

"About ten minutes. I'll go start the fries."

Lexie snagged a piece of cheese off the plate as he left to tide her over. She walked out from under the awning, enjoying the cool water on her bare feet. Last night was largely a blur, and she barely remembered sitting on the deck with Kade. They'd talked about her grandmother, or at least she thought they had.

Now that she was sober, she looked around, curious about Kade's home. Several yards from the deck, a small lake shimmered in the weak rays of sun that were poking through the clouds. The water was choppy from the storm and lapped at the shore in a soothing rhythm.

She did a double-take when she looked to the left. An enormous gray, two-story house with white columns along the front and a balcony that ran the whole length of it sat on a higher point of the property than Kade's house. At least she assumed that the two were on the same property. Even from this distance, the elegance of the place was quite intimidating.

Kade came back outside. "Okay. We'll be eating as soon as the bell dings."

Lexie flapped her hand in the mansion's direction. "Kade, whose house is that?"

Kade looked where she'd gestured. "Oh, that's mine."

Kade's writing career must be successful, but then hadn't his parent's had money? "Um, then why are you living here?"

"It's being renovated. This is my guesthouse."

Perplexed, Lexie asked, "It must be nice to be so rich."

"I worked hard for everything I have."

His reply confused Lexie even further. "But your family was rich."

Kade flashed a grin. "I gave most of my inheritance to Pastor Sal and the mission. I wanted to make my own money. Or maybe I was scared what that privilege would do to me. Look at Jason…"

"Everything did seem to come very easy for him. I don't think he knew the word no."

"Thinking I was above everyone else almost destroyed me. Pastor Sal showed me it's not money that makes a man, but his actions, and what he does in life," Kade said. "I think that's why my books sell so well, I'm grounded in the real world."

"Unlike Jason."

"Yeah," Kade replied.

"We couldn't avoid talking about him forever," Lexie said.

Kade started taking the burgers off the grill. "Let's not spoil dinner."

Lexie blew out a breath and nodded. She also realized that she wanted to get to know Kade a lot better. It became clear to her that other than sharing DNA and a love for car racing, Kade was very different than his younger brother. His brother thought of nothing but his own pleasure.

"Okay, we're ready. Let's eat."

"You don't have to tell me twice."

Lexie followed Kade like a rat following the Pied Piper. They ate at his kitchen table, which sat near the French doors, giving them a nice view of the lake. Throughout their scrumptious meal, she marveled at how much she was coming to care about Kade. It made her nervous because she'd been shying away from the idea of falling in love again. But deep in the pit of her stomach, she knew that she was fast approaching the danger zone with Kade.

Shoving away such troubling thoughts, Lexie was perfectly content to just enjoy being with him and living in the present.

Chapter Eighteen

A week later, Lexie was up early. She was picking Kade up to go running. She wore a new red and white sports bra and matching shorts that she'd splurged on since her other set was looking dingy.

She was getting her water bottle ready when someone knocked on the door. Thinking Kade was surprising her, Lexie smiled as she pulled the door open. "What are you..."

Her words died away when she saw Jason lounging against the doorjamb. The lopsided smile that had once made her heart race made her stomach curdle.

Pure fury swept through her, and before she knew it, her hand connect with Jason's cheek in a loud slap. A red splotch appeared on his cheekbone, satisfying Lexie's bent up anger and pain a bit.

"What the fuck?" His blue eyes blazed with anger and confusion.

Lexie forced herself to keep her hands at her sides so she didn't hit him again. "What? Were you expecting a warm welcome after all the shit you pulled on me? I can't stand the sight of you! All I want from you is my money and a signature. Sign the divorce papers and give me back my money, or I'll—"

Lexie slammed the door in his face and stood shaking with rage and pain as all the misery he'd put her through resurfaced. She knew she couldn't report him to the police, so best she not threaten that.

There was another knock, and Jason's voice came through the door. "Lex, I know I screwed up, but I'm not the same guy. Give me a chance to explain. I have some money for you."

Lexie wanted to tell him to go to hell, but the possibility of getting some much-needed money from the asshole made her reconsider.

She yanked the door open and glared at him. "How much money? Enough to save my cabin?"

Jason's triumphant smile made her want to punch him again. "I knew that would get your attention. I can give you a check for twenty-five hundred, and I'll talk to Kade about getting your loan repaid."

That wouldn't come close to paying the mortgage backlog, but it was better than nothing. Lexie crossed her arms. "No check. Cash only. I don't want to take a chance that it'll bounce. And you need to sign the divorce papers."

His expression darkened. "I'm not signing anything. I want to work things out."

Lexie let out a sarcastic laugh. "There's nothing to work out. It's over. I'm over *you*. I want to make a clean break and get on with my life."

Giving her a coaxing smile, Jason stepped closer. "C'mon, Lex. You don't mean that. I know you still love me."

She really didn't. Tears burned behind Lexie's eyes, but she didn't let them show. Tears never moved Jason. "You're wrong. You killed any love I ever had for you. I see now that I had stars in my eyes when we got married. It didn't take long before I discovered what kind of man you really are, though. But I put up with it because I loved you so much and thought you would change for me. I was an idiot. I tried to ignore all the times you cheated on me, but the drugs and you draining our bank accounts to support your habit was just too much.

"And when you stole from me by mortgaging the cabin," she swallowed hard, "any feelings I had left for you died. So there's nothing to work out except the terms of the divorce. Pay me back my money, sign the papers, and we can go our separate ways."

"Look at me. Can't you see?" Jason's eyes filled with regret. "Lexie, I know how much I screwed up, but I'm not the same guy. I'm clean. In fact, I just got out of rehab, and I haven't gotten high once or even touched booze. I have a sponsor and everything. That's what I spent the money on, the best rehab in the country."

Lexie said, "I've heard you sing that tune too many times, so forgive me if I don't sing along this time."

Jason moved closer, and the only effect he had on her was that she wanted to back away from him.

"This is different," he insisted. "I OD'd and almost died. It was a hell of a wake-up call. I decided right then to go to rehab." He rested a hand on her shoulder. "I'm sober, and that's the way I'm going to stay, no matter what it takes."

Lexie eased out from under his touch. The sincerity in his eyes and voice was unmistakable, and she wanted to believe him this time—for his sake and Kade's. It didn't matter, though. She wasn't the same person, either. The woman who'd been in love with Jason was gone, replaced by a stronger, wiser one, who was too smart to ever go back. It was too late.

"Jason, I'm glad you really seem to want to turn your life around, but I don't want to stay married to you. It's too late for any kind of reconciliation. I'll never forget about all the cheating you've done, all the pain you've put me through. So please, really hear me when I say it's over."

Jason backed off and nodded. "I hear you—but your thing with Kade factors into this, right?"

Lexie's breath hitched and her eyes went wide. He'd caught her off-guard.

He laughed, and the sarcastic sound raised her ire. "Did you think I wouldn't find out? Kade and I have mutual friends, remember?"

Lexie's temper spiked higher. "My life is none of your business. You gave up that right the day you left me."

He waggled a finger at her. "Last I checked, we're still married." His smile turned snarky. "Isn't it weird, screwing my brother?"

"And you wonder why I don't want to take you back," she said through clenched teeth. "We don't want to hurt you, but my relationship with Kade is none of your business."

Jason laughed again, apparently amused by her reaction.

"You haven't changed at all. You might not get high anymore, but you're still as much of an asshole as you always were." Yet his words had found their mark, goddamn it. She felt guilty.

Jason's smug expression infuriated her even more. "Have a good day, Lexie. See you around."

Lexie watched him walk to his car with her stomach churning. She should warn Kade.

Jason peeled away from the curb and Lexie went inside. She stood in her living room, shaking with anger over the encounter. Hating herself for giving him the satisfaction of rising to his bait.

She glanced at the clock. She'd be late meeting Kade now. The happiness of spending the morning with him faded. They both knew this day would come. She didn't know what she had been expecting, but not Jason sober and wanting her back in his life. He didn't love her. To him, she was merely a possession.

She walked to her car, wondering if she'd been wrong to get involved with Kade, but deep in her heart she was glad. Being with Kade was the only time she'd been happy in years.

She just hoped he didn't lose his brother over her. Would he resent her in the future?

Kade tapped his pen against his kitchen table as he reviewed the outline he'd just finished for an article on a new NASCAR model that Ford was working on for next year. It needed some tweaking, but that was nothing new. He never wasted a lot of time on detailed outlines because he always ended up switching the order around.

Although it took longer, he often preferred doing rough drafts old school. There was something about working with pen and paper that stirred his creative juices. He grabbed a clean sheet of paper and started on a second draft of the outline.

A knock on the doorjamb of the kitchen door interrupted him. Looking up, he saw Lexie standing there with an odd look on her face. He hadn't heard her arrive.

He got up and warily approached her. "Hey, babe. I lost track of time. I'll be ready in a sec." He tried to kiss her, but she avoided him. "Is something wrong?"

"That depends."

Kade cocked an eyebrow at her cryptic reply. "Okay. What's going on?" He motioned towards the living room, but Lexie stayed put.

She lifted her chin, her gaze guarded. "Jason showed up at my place this morning."

A jolt of surprise ran through Kade, but he just frowned. "Is he okay? And what did he want?"

Lexie sighed. "He seems fine—good health, too. He claims he's been in rehab. He changed after a near-death experience. The funny thing is… I believe him this time. But he's just as much of a tool as he ever was. He's refusing to sign the divorce papers. And of course the money is gone."

Kade pulled her into his arms, but she held herself stiffly. "I told you I'd give you the money."

"He knows about us. And he's pissed." She looked into his eyes. "I don't know why. He doesn't really love me. I suspect he's terrified of the 'where to go from here' and I'm familiar."

She pushed out of his arms. "I think we should cool things down while we get this sorted. I don't want our relationship used as an excuse to push him back into drugs."

Going to the fridge, Kade got out a bottle of water and twisted off the cap. "If he *is* clean, I want him to stay that way, too, but I don't want to put my life on hold or deny my love for you. I'll talk to him. Did he say where he was staying?"

She shook her head. "No."

Going to her, Kade slid his arms around her waist. "You'll see. I'll talk with Jason and get everything sorted. I won't let him hurt you ever again."

"I hope you're right."

"Let's go for that run. Burn off all this nervous energy. We can't do anything more until Jason gets in touch again. Let me go to the bank and pay the loan off. Once this situation is done and dusted, I'm looking forward to you and I spending a long week in this cabin. I'd love you to share your memories of your time there... and we could make some of our own."

Thankfully, his words pacified her. But as he was getting changed into his running gear, he wondered if it would be as simple as he made it sound.

Chapter Nineteen

A few days later, at work, after finishing up changing brake pads and rotating some tires, Lexie took her tools to her rolling tool chest. On a table next to it, there was a small basin of Dawn water and another that held rinse water. The guys teased her about it sometimes, but Lexie was fanatical about keeping her tools clean since she couldn't afford to buy more.

She started washing her socket wrench, concentrating on removing the grease from each of the grooves. A shadow fell over her, and she looked up to see Marcus standing there. Unease slid through her veins because it was rare for him to approach her except in passing.

"You busy?" he asked.

"I'm cleaning these, and then I'm helping Sully with a couple things, so, yeah, I'm busy."

One side of Marcus' mouth lifted. "Sully can wait. I need to talk with you."

Lexie's heart rate went up. "Why?"

His small smile disappeared. "In my office would be best."

He turned and walked away, and Lexie hurriedly finished washing her socket wrench and let it sit out to air dry. Refusing to trot after him like a little puppy, Lexie walked at a regular pace while watching him enter the office. When she went inside, he had his butt perched on his desk.

"So, we're gonna talk about your job performance." He held up a silencing hand when Lexie bristled. "When Tom hired you, you know I wasn't happy."

"Pffft! Not happy? You were pissed as hell. I've worked my ass off to justify him hiring me," Lexie responded.

Marcus' gaze intensified. "I know."

Lexie glared at him, but she remained silent.

He sighed and motioned to the chair that sat by his desk and then took his own. Once Lexie sat down, he said, "You're right. I wanted to kill Tom for bringing you on, but I'm glad now that he did."

Did she just hear him correctly? Her expression must've said it all because Marcus let out a shout of laughter. "Wow, I totally shocked the shit out of you."

"That's like the mother of all understatements."

"I like keeping you on your toes."

Lexie's temper rose. "I know."

"Okay, okay. I'll get on with it," Marcus said, pulling open one of his drawers. He pulled out a folded piece of paper and slid it across the desk to her.

Lexie glanced at it and then at him. "I guess it's not a pink slip. It's the wrong color."

Marcus smiled. "Look at it."

As she reached for it, Lexie was as leery about what it contained as she was about touching a snake. She unfolded it to find the numerals for twenty percent written in large letters on the page.

She shook her head a little. "What does this mean?"

"It's your raise. Twenty percent more a year, starting two months ago."

Lexie's heart lurched, and she felt so faint she put a hand on the desk to keep from falling off her chair. "What?" Her voice came out in a hoarse squeak, and she cleared her throat. "What did you just say?"

"And that ain't all, folks," Marcus said in a game show host's voice. "Let's see what else Lexie has won!"

In a daze, Lexie watched him set an envelope on the desk.

"Open it."

Somehow, she kept the trembling in her hands to a minimum as she picked it up and ripped the envelope. She pulled out a Bad Boy Autos check—and gasped at the amount printed on it. "Te—ten th—ousand dollars?" She counted the zeroes, sure that her eyes were doing funky shit. "Ten thousand dollars?"

"Yeah. You netted us some serious profit over the last three months with not just your mechanical work, but your detailing work, too. In fact," his TV host voice came back, "let's go see what's behind door number three!"

Lexie couldn't move at first, but Marcus' order to get off her butt and follow him did the trick. The smell of stale coffee hit as they moved through the break room into the cavern of grease-monkey heaven that was the supply warehouse. She almost ran smack into Marcus' back because he'd stopped.

"You wanted to show me the supply closet?"

He opened the door and turned on the light. "Welcome to your new office."

Peering around him, all Lexie saw was brooms, buckets, cleaning supplies and other odds and ends. "It's the supply closet, not an office."

"True, but it *will* be an office soon, and you'll help design it."

She put a hand on his arm. "I don't understand. Why do I need an office?"

Marcus turned the light off and shut the door. "Day after day, I watch you draw in the break room or in the garage on that table. The designs you create are freaking amazing. I've seen my parents buy art that's supposedly worth thousands of dollars that doesn't come close to what you do. You need a proper place to do your work, Lexie. That's how good I think it is. I always have."

"Okay, you are super freaking me out right now," Lexie said.

Marcus' grin drew a smile from her. "I can see that."

"I didn't realize you liked my design work so much."

His expression sobered. "At the risk of sounding like a wuss, this place is precious to me, Lexie. There's no way in hell I'd accept inferior work here. Ever. Your work is the best I've ever seen, and it's getting noticed. It will bring in more business.

"You deserve that raise and a work office where you can design your ass off. And whatever clients you bring in, you'll get a commission on. I haven't run the numbers yet, but we can figure that out later."

Marcus' praise and friendly attitude with Lexie was so strange, she was certain she'd been transported to a parallel universe where everything was opposite to this one. *Fringe on steroids*, she thought. Between that, the pay raise and the check he'd handed her, Lexie couldn't hold back her emotions.

She clutched the check to her chest as tears flooded her eyes and she tried to speak. However, she couldn't even manage a whisper. Holding up the check, she nodded and gave a thumbs-up sign before a sob slipped out. She could pay off most of her debts if this kept up.

Marcus' black eyebrows knitted, and he put his hands on his hips. "Why are you crying? You don't cry. At least, I've never seen you cry. I don't like it. Stop it."

Laughter bubbled up to mingle with her tears over his reaction. A huge hiccup escaped her, and she covered her mouth to muffle another one.

"Damn it." Marcus tentatively embraced Lexie as though she were a bomb he expected to explode at any moment.

This further amused Lexie, making her sobs change over completely to laughter. But she put her arms around his waist, grateful beyond words to Marcus for his generosity. It seemed like he wasn't the complete tool she'd thought.

Marcus gave her a squeeze before releasing her and holding her at arm's length. "Well, at least you're not crying anymore. You okay?"

Lexie nodded and used the sleeve of her overalls to wipe away her tears. "Sorry. It's just that you don't understand how much this means to me. It'll go a long way towards paying off my bills. Thank you."

"You're welcome, but I want to clarify that I'm not doing this out of pity. You earned it. I always reward good work," Marcus said.

Back in control, Lexie smiled. "I'm glad to hear that. I wouldn't take the money if I thought you felt sorry for me."

Marcus grimaced a little. "Well, I'm sorry that you had to put up with a scumbag like Jason for so long, but I don't pity you. He's an idiot for not appreciating what he had, but it's nice that Kade does."

"What do you know about that?" Lexie narrowed her eyes. "Has Tom been talking to you about me?"

"No, but I have eyes, Lexie. I see how he looks at you every time he comes here. It's easy to see he's really into you. Kade's a good guy. He's a straight shooter and he doesn't play games. Besides that, he's responsible and has a good work ethic."

Lexie laughed. "Are you trying to sell me on him?"

Marcus shrugged. "No, just telling you what I think."

"All right. I'll take that under advisement. And I'll add that Stella's a great woman, too."

"Stella? What's that mean?"

She smiled, loving being back in the driver's seat with Marcus. "Sssh. I'll keep your secret. I saw you kissing her a few nights ago."

"You must have been mistaken."

"Nope. Don't worry, I've told no one."

"Good. Just mind your business." He made a shooing motion. "Okay, back to work."

Lexie thanked him again and went to her locker. Before she

stowed the check that Marcus had given her in her backpack, she looked at it for a few moments. Both the check and the raise were life changing for her. And Jason wouldn't get his hands on any of it. He had no right to it.

A wave of panic hit her, and she suddenly needed to have Tom deposit it in her secret account right that second. Then she berated herself for being so silly. It could wait until after work.

Her excitement returned as she realized her money woes were closer to being over, thanks to Marcus.

Unbidden, Kade came to mind, and she felt a strong impulse to call him, to tell him the fantastic news. He was the first person she wanted to tell.

"You gonna come help me with that Chevy or stand here daydreaming all day?"

Coming back to herself, she looked up at Sully. "Yeah, sure."

An amused glint entered his eyes. "'Yeah, sure,' you're going to come help me, or yeah, sure,' you're gonna daydream some more?"

Lexie laughed and closed her locker. "I'll help you. I have to make sure you don't screw up that carburetor."

"Listen, I've been fixing carburetors since before you were out of diapers."

"I know, Silver Fox, but older doesn't always mean better."

"When it comes to me, it does."

Bursting into laughter, Lexie followed him back to the garage.

Chapter Twenty

Kade found a parking spot down the road from the bank. He couldn't wait to get the cabin back for Lexie. He knew how much it meant to her. The way her eyes shined when she spoke of her time there with her mother's boyfriend Nick and her mother, Clara. He wished he could have met her mother.

His hand was on the door handle when his mobile rang. About to send it to voice mail, the number on the screen saw him pressing answer instead.

"Hi, Kade. Long time no see."

"How are you, Charlie?" His mouth firmed. What could Charlie Erickson want with him? He hoped he hadn't heard about the story Kade was about to sell to a major newspaper in LA. It would probably lead to an FBI investigation into the Erickson racing team.

"I've been better. A little birdie tells me you have some information that you shouldn't have. It will get nasty if that information ever sees the light of day."

"A story is never nasty if it's the truth."

"Tsk, tsk. Don't you know that sometimes the truth hurts?

Take your little visit to the bank today. I wouldn't bother getting out of the car."

He peered through the windscreen and let his gaze sweep the streets. Was Charlie spying on him?

Charlie continued. "I already bought your girlfriend's lovely little cabin from the bank."

Kade's blood ran cold. "What? You're lying. She has until five p.m. today."

"Whoops, the bank foreclosure documents said five p.m. yesterday."

"They bloody did not." Kade gripped the steering wheel until his knuckles went white. Somehow Charlie had managed to fraudulently change the date on the foreclosure documents. That would never stand up in court, but now it would be a huge ugly fight. Lexie didn't need this. "What do you want?"

"Give us the evidence you have and we'll sell you back the cabin."

At an exorbitant price, no doubt. He was about to agree. He could always write his story another time. Wait for a few months and gather more evidence.

Then Charlie said, "And you're going to do the next delivery over the border for us. And we'll have the evidence of you doing it. You can't write a story that implicates yourself. Try explaining that away. You'd be ruined."

He wished he had a punching bag in the car with him, or better yet, Charlie's smug face. There was no way in hell he would do that. The Erikson's had underestimated him. He would not let Lexie lose the cabin this way, no matter how much it cost him to fight this.

"Don't wait too long to decide. I might feel like selling the cabin," and then the phone went dead.

He rested his head on the steering wheel. Shit. What was he going to tell Lexie? He wasn't stupid. No way would he agree to take stolen parts across the border for the Ericksons. If he was caught—and he wouldn't put it past the Ericksons to make that happen—life as he knew it would be over. He'd be in jail. His hand went to his phone to call his lawyer. Could they investigate the fraud with the bank? There must be a money trail on which staff member they'd paid off.

Once he'd finished talking to his lawyer, and started the process of investigation, he knew who he had to see—Lexie.

Lexie would understand what had just happened. Or would she blame him? Another Colter had stuffed up. He'd underestimated the Erickson's and potentially cost her the one thing he'd promised to protect—her cabin. His lawyer said it would take a long time to fight this and by then they could have sold the cabin to anyone several times over. Even if they won the case, it's likely she'd only receive compensation, not the cabin.

Lexie was expecting the cabin ownership papers to be in her hands tonight. What was he going to do now?

Chapter Twenty-One

After work, Lexie got in her Jeep and took her phone out of her backpack. She drummed her fingers on the steering wheel as she tried to decide whether to call Kade or pop by his place.

She missed Kade. Silly really, she'd only seen him that morning.

A smile spread over her face as she realized that falling in love again didn't scare the shit out of her anymore. She wouldn't rush into it, but there was no reason not to enjoy being with Kade in the meantime.

Her smile faded when she thought about the fact Jason would not sign the papers, yet he wasn't coming at her for anything. He wasn't begging her to come back to him. He wasn't asking for money. What was he up to?

His silence made her nervous. Perhaps he was expecting Kade to pay up. He had the money. And really, brothers looked out for each other. She could hardly blame Kade for wanting to help Jason get back on his feet. Kade wasn't stupid enough to give Jason money without ensuring he didn't go back on the drugs.

She'd go home and have a long, hot bath and plan a surprise

trip for Kade up to her cabin. He should have paid back the money this afternoon. With her recent promotion and the chance at commission on her work, she'd make a plan with Kade to pay back every penny. It would be easier with no interest. A trip to the cabin would be good for both of them. It would be wonderful to share her memories of the only happy place she'd lived after her mother got out of rehab.

She'd been fifteen, and they'd moved up there after they'd released Lexie from foster care. They had a wonderful twelve months living by the lake before her mother got sick. Nick, her mother's partner, the man who'd helped her get clean, had stood by them both.

It had taken her mom another twelve months to die. Only Nick kept Lexie sane, and he helped her get a job working on cars. He'd given her the bug by letting her work on his Chevy. He was the one who'd told her she had a natural talent with engines and helped her get started. It was Tom who got her a job working on the racing circuit.

She smiled at the memory. Tom had thought she was hot, and he'd only given her a job because he'd wanted to get into her pants. But they soon realized their friendship was more important than a quick fuck. Plus, Tom said he didn't want to lose a great mechanic.

Nick died in a car accident two years ago, and now the cabin was hers. She couldn't wait to share the beautiful spot by the lake with Kade. She hoped he wouldn't think the cabin too rustic.

Suddenly, she didn't want a bath. She wanted Kade. She wanted to share today with the man who was slowly owning her heart.

"This is a nice surprise," he muttered as he opened the door to her. She merely launched herself into his arms and kissed him. He kissed her back, and the urgency in his touch sent her pulse racing.

With a primal growl that sent shivers through her, Kade claimed her lips, urging them apart as he slammed the door shut behind her with his foot. Lexie gave in, gliding her tongue against his in a sensual dance. She moaned when he pulled her hips tight against him, fitting her body to his.

His growing erection rubbed against her stomach, and the urge to touch him was too much to resist. Slipping a hand between them, Lexie found the button on the waistband of his jeans and undid it.

When his hand halted hers, she looked up in surprise. "I have something I need to tell you first."

She pressed a kiss to his lips to silence him. "It can wait. I need you."

She slid her hand inside, fondling him through his underwear. Sex with Kade was amazing, but feeling and seeing the evidence of how much she excited him was one part she loved most. She didn't like to admit it, but she needed that validation.

"Wait. We have to—"

"It doesn't feel like you want to talk," judging by how hard he was. His cock jutted towards her as though it yearned for her touch. She supposed it did, because the rest of Kade seemed to. On a groan he gave in.

His hand fisted in her hair and the other was working its way up under the back of her t-shirt. Her skin broke out in goose bumps and her nipples pebbled against his chest when she felt his warm palm connect with her bare back.

Kade dragged his lips from hers, leaving her dazed and breathless. "I want you. Now."

Her arousal grew stronger as she stared at him. Her breasts felt heavier, and she ached with desire. She wanted him as much as he did her, so she settled for committing the moment to memory. The hot glint in his eyes, the rapid way his chest rose and fell, and his proud, erect penis—all burned into her brain.

"You're overdressed. Let's fix that." And he lifted her t-shirt over her head. "You are so beautiful it hurts."

Never had Lexie felt so wanted, so needed as a woman, as a *person*. No other man had ever said that to her, had ever felt that way about her, but Kade did. And he might have a granite-like hard-on at the moment, but it was easy to see that he was talking about more than sex.

"How am I supposed to get naked with you latched onto me like that?"

The barest hint of a smile played around Kade's mouth before he kissed her hard and then released her. She pulled off her shirt and got rid of her hot-purple yoga shorts. For a moment, Lexie wished she was wearing a sexier bra and panties instead of her white sports bra and boy shorts. Then she caught the way Kade was looking at her and realized she didn't need fancy clothes to make him want her.

She ran her fingers under the bottom of the bra, teasing Kade by not lifting the bra quite all the way up. His nostrils flared and he shifted on his feet. She toyed with her bra a little longer, but the sight of his delectable body made her as impatient as he was.

She rid herself of the bra and the panties soon followed. Standing bared to the elements with Kade was a huge aphrodisiac. The breeze caressed her, a hint of erotic contact, and the lingering sun kissed her skin. They were a tiny prelude to what she knew was in store for her.

Hunger stamped his chiseled features as his eyes traveled over her. Lexie stepped up to him and hooked a hand around the back of his neck. They stared into each other's eyes for several moments before Kade ran his hands over her buttocks and up her back. He traced her spine and she shuddered in delight.

Bringing his hands around, he filled them with her breasts and bent down to take a pink tip in his mouth. Watching him suck and run his tongue around her nipple made the heavenly sensations even stronger. He kissed his way over to her other breast, and she sighed as he sucked hard on her nipple.

She couldn't hold still as excitement built. Kade released her and gave her a knowing smile as he started backing over to one of the large chairs. He pulled her along with him and sat down on it.

"Come on, baby. Wanna go for a ride?"

The husky timber in his voice and the way he looked stretched out on the chair had Lexie practically salivating. "Well, I do enjoy driving stick."

"Then get a move on."

Lifting a leg, Lexie swung over and straddled his hips. She sat down on his thighs but didn't take him inside. Instead, she ran her fingers over his rigid shaft, loving the way his eyes darkened and the restless shift of his hips. Enjoying her power over him, Lexie inched up his body, brushing her mound over his cock.

Kade groaned, the sound vibrating under her hands as Lexie leaned forward. "You're killing me here, Lex, and you know it."

She laughed as she said, "Oh, yeah, and I'm loving every second of it."

Reaching down, she grasped him and guided him to her entrance. Slowly, she sat down, enjoying the sensation of him gradually filling her. They breathed a collective sigh when she took him inside her.

Resting his hands on Lexie's thighs, Kade was mesmerized by her beauty. The sun brought out the burnished gold highlights in her hair and turned her eyes from chocolate to coffee. Anytime they made love was amazing, but he preferred it in the daytime so he could enjoy her in the natural light. Never had a woman turned him on so much, and he knew that he'd never get his fill of her.

He also knew he was being a jerk. He should have told her about the cabin the minute she'd arrived, but the urge to make love to her took over. If she hated him and left...

Looking at where they were joined, Kade thought it was almost as though they were one. Almost. She wasn't on the same page as his heart, but he felt like she was only a few pages behind. He hoped she was, or else losing the cabin might destroy them.

His heart might be willing to wait, but his body was another matter. Her warm, wet sheath tightened around him as she leaned forward and pressed her lips to his. She ran her tongue over his bottom lip, and his libido shifted into overdrive. He kissed her back, sweeping his tongue into her mouth. Raising his hips, he urged her to move.

She chuckled against his mouth and then let out a squeal when he gave her a hard bump. She broke the kiss and rested her forehead against his. Her expression had turned fierce and determined. "Hard and fast."

The short, forceful sentence told Kade all he needed to know. That's how it was with Lexie, and he loved never having to guess. "Fine by me."

She rose and came back down, sliding along his length. Then the ride really started. Her toned thighs flexed as she began a rhythm that quickly increased. Kade's blood sizzled through his veins as she rose and fell. Her breasts followed her movements, and he couldn't resist reaching out to palm them.

He caressed and kneaded them, but when he started rubbing her nipples with his thumbs, Lexie moaned. "Just like that," she murmured, her voice husky from passion.

Kade clamped down on his need for release and concentrated on Lexie. He wanted to make her scream, to brand himself on her soul. He wanted to show her how much he loved her, and there was no better way to do that than to give her what she wanted, how she needed it.

Continuing to rub the pads of his thumbs across her taut nipples, he asked, "Just like that?"

"Yes."

"What will happen if I do?"

A moan rose from her throat.

"Will you come for me?"

"Oh god."

"Will you?"

"Yes!"

"Good. You feel so good, babe…"

The more he talked to her, the more urgent her movements grew. She trembled and strained towards her goal. He could tell that she was almost there, and he wanted to help her reach her goal, to give her the pleasure she sought.

Running his right hand down her body, he found her sex and brushed his thumb over her clitoris.

She switched to a rocking motion that created greater friction and had him sucking in a breath. The new angle intensified the pleasurable sensations coursing through his body, and he almost lost control. It was tested even further when the first pulses of her release began. Her hips moved against his in a frantic pace, and she cried out. She dropped her head forward and froze.

Kade watched with pride and amazement as she came. Her mouth hung open a little and tremors shook her as bliss filled her face. Her orgasm ended on a high-pitched, shuddering moan that faded into heavy breathing.

"That was incredible."

Kade kissed her and lay back on the chair. "I'm glad, but you better hang on tight. That was just the warm-up lap, now the race is on."

He positioned Lexie where he wanted her and started thrusting, long, deep strokes that gave her a few moments to recover. But it wasn't long before he set a blistering pace. Over and over, he drove into her, loving the little mewling cries that came from the back of her throat.

But when she leaned forward and bit his shoulder, it sent him into a frenzy. Wrapping an arm around her waist and bracing his feet on the chair, he started thrusting even faster, driving them both towards completion at breakneck speed.

"Yes, Kade! Yes, yes…"

Her words became a litany, an almost incoherent string of words as he felt her climax again. This time while she contracted around him, Kade followed her. Her voice rose in a crescendo, and he let out a loud groan as a powerful wave of ecstasy crashed down on him. He gave one last thrust as Lexie quaked against him.

Holding on to each other, they rode around the far turn and sailed across the finish line. Their mutual release was so intense that neither could speak nor move once the rapture of the moment began fading. Lexie flopped down on him, and he kissed her temple and caressed her back. They lay like that for several minutes before Lexie raised her head and stared into his eyes.

He smiled and brushed hair back from her face. "You are the most incredible woman I've ever known."

The blush that stained her cheeks was endearing, because Lexie didn't blush easily. He'd seen tons of guys compliment her, but she'd never reacted to them that way. It made him feel good to know that he affected her.

Sliding her arms around his neck, she cupped the back of his head, loving the feel of his smooth skin. "Do you have any idea what an awesome guy you are?"

His mouth quirked up in a smug smile. "Maybe a little."

She tweaked his ear. "Stop that. I'm being serious here."

Embracing her, he kissed her nose. "Sorry. You were saying?"

"I know there are good guys out there, but after Jason, I didn't have any hope of ever meeting one. Then you turned up with that car and showed me that good men do exist. From the first time you took me out, you treated me with respect and kindness." She traced the line of his strong jaw with her fingers. "You make me so happy that sometimes I feel like I'm dreaming. You're all I could ever ask for in a man...and I love you so much."

His eyes went wide, and his breathing came faster. "Lexie, don't say it just because you're lost in the euphoria of great sex."

"Not sex, making love." Taking his face in her hands, Lexie said, "I love you."

Kade examined her face for a few moments. He settled his lips over hers in a slow, sweet, devastating kiss that ignited her hunger for him.

Pulling back, he smiled into her eyes. "Tell me again."

"I love you, Kade."

His hands started roaming over her, and Lexie wanted him with an intensity that left her feeling a little lightheaded. "I love you, too, Lex. But we really do need to talk."

She laughed. "I don't have the energy to talk right now."

"It's important." She snuggled closer. "It's about the cabin."

Something in his voice alerted her, and her eyes flew open. "You went to the bank today?"

"Sort of." With that, he moved her off him and rose, walking to pull his jeans on. "Get dressed and I'll make us a drink. You'll need it."

Her heart slowed as her guts churned. Something was wrong.

She scrambled into her clothes and followed him into the kitchen. His hands were shaking. "What about my cabin?"

"When I got there, someone else had already bought it."

Her breath choked in her throat. She wrapped her arms around herself to beat back the pain. "No. I had until five p.m." She whirled on him. "Were you late? Did you mess this up? How could you?"

He pulled her into his arms and she beat at his chest. "No. I was there at two p.m. But it is because of me. Sit down and I'll explain."

She sat on his couch in his arms as he told her the story. Each word taking a piece of her new happiness with her. When he'd finished, she wiped the tears from her face.

"Pease don't cry. I have my lawyer and investigation team working on how we stop this and try to get the cabin back."

"But even if we prove wrong doing the cabin could be gone."

"Yes. I'm so sorry. Can you ever forgive me?"

She wanted to say, "it's not your fault." She wanted to scream at the injustice of having the cabin almost in her grasp, only to have it taken away again—by something a Colter did. She knew that wasn't fair, but she could hardly breathe through the pain.

She pushed to her feet. Her head was pounding, and she felt ill.

"I need to go. I need to process all of this." She looked down at him and tears fell. "I don't want to blame you. I know it's not really your fault, but I've just lost the most important thing in my life and I… I need some time to grieve."

"I thought *I* might be the most important thing in your life."

His hurt pierced her heart and made her feel about an inch tall.

She couldn't answer him, so she turned and fled.

Chapter Twenty-Two

K ade was on a mission. He'd worked through his contacts and found out that Jason was staying with one of his buddies who lived in East LA. After the disaster of the cabin, he'd ensure Jason divorced her with no further drama. He owed her that.

Weariness weighed him down. He wished he'd paid off the mortgage when he'd first suggested it to Lexie. If he had, she wouldn't have shut him out of her life. His heart wouldn't have a shattered hollow in his chest.

Why couldn't she love me enough?

His mind argued with itself—she loves me, she loves me not. Deep down, he knew she no longer loved his brother, but that didn't mean she loved him either. Pain made him irrational, and he hoped he could be civil to Jason.

He'd not heard from Lexie in days, and it was so hard not to go to her and beg her to take him back, but he'd give her the space she'd asked for, scared she might leave for good. He needed space, too. He couldn't forget the pain that had swamped him when she'd walked out, proving she loved her cabin more than him.

Driving down the street, Kade rehearsed what he would say

to Jason as he looked for the right building. He spied a parking spot and quickly swung into it.

Getting out, he locked his car and strode toward the tall brick building with purposeful steps. He ran up the stairs to the third floor and knocked on the door of apartment 18. It opened, and Jason stood there. He looked haggard, and thinner than the last time Kade had seen him.

"I wondered when you'd get around to finding me." Jason stepped back, opening the door wider. "C'mon in, bro."

Kade stepped into the kitchen of the apartment and looked around. The place was dated, but surprisingly clean. The wood-paneled walls made the small room seem dark, and the faded green floral linoleum had seen better days. However, the appliances and single window sparkled.

"You want a beer?"

Kade shook his head. "No. I want you to sign your divorce papers. Lexie doesn't want you back."

Jason took a Coke from the refrigerator and twisted off the top.

"Still sober?" Kade said.

Jason leaned against the counter and took a swig of his drink. "I'm off drugs and booze."

"I'm hoping the brother I used to know and love is around today, because I'm here to beg you to give Lexie the divorce she wants."

Silence fell between them as Jason met Kade's plea-filled gaze. At length, he said, "You love her, don't you?"

"More than life." Kade didn't feel shy about admitting it. "Can you say that you ever loved her like that?"

The regret in Jason's smile surprised Kade. "No. I can't. I should've done us both a favor and never put a ring on her finger. She's one hell of a woman, but I'm not in love with her. I don't think I ever was. I wasn't capable of loving anyone but myself."

Kade smiled. "That's quite an insight."

Jason nodded sagely. "You're right, but enough about that. The only reason you want me to sign the divorce papers is because you want to marry her. Am I right?"

Kade didn't deny it. "Yeah. But I don't think that will happen anytime soon."

"How come?"

At Jason's puzzled frown, Kade sat on the kitchen stool and told him the story about the Ericksons.

"That funkin' sucks, man. Charlie and Jack always were douchebags." He looked at Kade and sighed. "It's really my fault. If I hadn't mortgaged the property…"

"What's done is done. I'm holding off sending in the story in to make them think I'm going to play along but I have a team working on the problem. But I admit, the chance of getting her cabin back is slim."

"You mean get Lexie back," Jason said.

"I wish. The cabin is a good start." They looked at each other, both full of guilt. "Anyway, will you sign the papers?"

"Sure. I should have signed them weeks ago but—but I was scared. Signing the papers means I really am starting at the beginning again. I just needed to be sure it wouldn't send me spiraling downwards again. It's a slippery slope and a battlefield I walk every day. I'm still scared…"

Kade really looked at his brother. He looked so tired. It must be tiring, this constant battle. "You have me." He was so lucky he didn't have any addictions—except Lexie. "I've been doing up the mansion. It's almost finished. The guesthouse is yours if you want it."

Jason stood up tall and took his hands out of his pockets. "You mean it? You'll let me live in the guesthouse?"

"As long as you stay off the drugs, it's yours."

"I will. If I go back—I'm dead. The drugs will kill me next time I know it."

"I don't want to lose my only brother, so you let me know if you need any help. In fact, I have some work for you. Research mostly, but your contacts in the racing world will come in helpful."

Jason's eyes filled with tears. "Thank you, Kade. I won't let you down. I promise."

Kade stood and they hugged each other. A weight lifted off Kade's heart. He hoped this meant he had his brother back. A more mature, wiser and humble brother.

No sooner had Kade left his apartment, Jason picked up the phone and dialed a number. "Mrs. Erickson, Jason Colter here. I was wondering if you had time for a visit this afternoon. You do? Wonderful. I'll see you at four p.m."

Chapter Twenty-Three

Sully knocked on Lexie's apartment door and looked around the neighborhood. It seemed nice enough, but he'd never live in a place like this. It was too cookie-cutter for him. He preferred his ancient house with all its quirks, the huge backyard and swimming pool. However, Lexie couldn't afford to be fussy.

When Lexie opened the door she wasn't surprised to see him.

"Look, I appreciate you stopping by, but I'm fine. I just need some time."

Sully put his hands on his hips. "You've had time. You need to get back to work. I need my partner back, and we've got two design jobs lined up."

Lexie nodded. "I know. I'm just—"

"Wallowing. That's what you're doing. Start doing what you love again. That's what you do when you get your head messed up," Sully said. "Bury yourself in work."

His attitude made her temper flare. "Is that what you did after your divorce?" she challenged.

Sully's face tightened, but he nodded. "Yep. It was a big part of what kept me from drinking myself to death. I've been down lower than you, sweetheart, but I clawed my way back. So, I'm speaking from experience when I say that you can do it, too. It's gonna hurt like hell, but you just take it one moment at a time."

"I'm just trying to work out what I want, and what I need. I know it was only a cabin, but it was all I had."

"Not all. You've got Kade."

"I know and he deserves someone who isn't broken and messed up."

"Ah, damn it. Can you try to forgive him? It really wasn't his fault about the cabin. You know you're blaming the wrong Colter."

"I do know that. It's more about me than him. I'm so messed up."

"Are you? The cabin is just wood and nails. Your mother lives in your memories and in your heart. I think that cabin is your crutch. With a man like Kade standing by your side, you don't need it. Love is all you need. And from what Kendra and Stella have told me, Kade loves you in spades. He's hurting, too."

A tiny piece of her knew Sully was right. But she'd had so little time with her mother, the cabin...

Suddenly, Sully was there. She squeezed her eyes shut and leaned against him as big, hot tears dripped onto her cheeks and soaked his shirt. It was the first time she'd cried over Kade, and agony battered her from all directions. She was too weak to resist as Sully guided her over to the couch and sat down with her.

He didn't talk, just held her while she poured out all of her heartache. Uncontrollable sobs wracked her body, and it felt like the river of tears would never dry up.

After a time, Sully pulled her back and said, "Hey, now, you gotta stop. You're gonna make yourself sick, girl."

Lexie shook her head as another sob shook her.

Sully grabbed her arms, threw back his head and shouted, *"She was a fast machine, she kept her motor clean!"*

Lexie immediately ceased crying and clapped a hand over his mouth. "Shut the hell up. Oh, my god, Sully."

He laughed behind her hand and pulled it away. "I knew that would get your attention. Now, look, I know that it will be a real bitch, but you have to come back. It will help, I swear.

"You've worked too hard to give up your dreams over a massive disappointment. You're stronger than that, and you got a lot of friends who'll help you through this. And a man who loves you if you'll let him. You know how rare that is?" He kissed the side of her head and got up. "So you quit your bawling, and get your ass to work tomorrow, or I'll be back to serenade you some more."

Gratitude for his kindness filled Lexie. "Thank you, Sully."

He gave her a stern look and shook his finger at her. "You just thank me by showing up tomorrow."

She grabbed a tissue from the box on the coffee table and blew her nose. "Okay."

"I'm holding you to that."

In her mind, she saw Sully singing again and started laughing, feeling lighter than she had since the debacle with Kade. Huffing out a sigh, she said, "Okay, Lexie, time to get your shit together."

And she had to go talk with Kade. He would be worried sick, blaming himself.

She was so stupid. Sully was right—it was only a cabin.

She gripped the locket around her neck. Her mother was wherever Lexie was, because she was in her heart. It was time to put the past behind her. And she needed her big girls' panties on to learn to trust again. Deep down, she knew Kade would never hurt her on purpose. He would always be there for her.

It suddenly seemed all so clear. She loved Kade and losing the cabin didn't change that.

Pulling her mobile out of her pocket, she dialed Kendra's number. "Hey, Kendra. Can you do me a favor? I want to plan a surprise dinner for Kade."

"Oh, wonderful! You've forgiven him."

"There really isn't anything to forgive. I owe him a huge apology for blaming him. So, can you help me organize this?"

"Sure. I'd love to. I'll get Stella to help. What do you want me to do?"

"Well, Sully told me Kade's moving back into his house on Friday. Stella's working on getting a spare key to Kade's house and I was wondering if you could get Tom to take him out for the afternoon, then you, Stella and I could set up a lovely surprise dinner."

"Sure, Tom will think of something. But what are you going to do?"

"I'll just dial in Stella. She'll have some ideas."

Soon after Lexie had explained that she wanted to surprise Kade, Stella was full of brilliant ideas. Stella outlined her plan, and soon the girls were giggling away.

K ade moved back into the big house on Friday morning, leaving the guesthouse for Jason. As he walked through the beautifully renovated mansion, he'd never felt more alone in the large, rambling rooms. Why did he need a house this size? He wanted to share it with Lexie—and have a family with her.

If only Lexie were here with him.

What hurt the most was that he loved Lexie more than she loved him. He wouldn't care if he lost everything he owned, as long as she was by his side. Yet, she couldn't forgive him one tiny cabin.

He knew that wasn't fair to her. He hadn't had her upbringing. He'd had a loving mother and father and led a privileged life. He hadn't been raised by a junkie mother, or ended up in foster care, only to have her mum return and then lose her to a terrible wasting disease. Nor had he had his self-respect and dignity trampled on by a drug-addict husband who'd left her destitute and then tossed her aside like garbage.

He understood what that cabin represented to her. He just hoped that if he could see her, touch her, she'd remember that he loved her and she'd forgive him.

He took one last look around before glancing at his watch. He was meeting Tom this afternoon, who had agreed to help him design a plan to get Lexie back.

Shit, he best move it. They were meeting at Tom's house, since he was looking after the kids today.

It took about twenty minutes to drive to Tom's, and he suddenly felt stupid. How the hell was Tom going to help him get Lexie to see him, let alone make her love him again?

Tom greeted him with no animosity, which surprised Kade. The man was Lexie's biggest fan. He handed Kade a beer as they sat outside on the porch.

"Nice house," he said.

"We like it. Now, let's hear it."

Smiling, Kade threw a ball for Connor, Tom's little boy. Ignoring the shard of sorrow that pierced his heart, Kade said, "I'd appreciate any help you can give me. I never meant to hurt Lexie. Just the opposite. It sounds dramatic, but I wanted to give her everything—the cabin would have been just the beginning."

"I get that," Tom said. "She's just grieving the loss. Give her time."

"I'm so angry with myself. I underestimated Charlie Erickson. I got careless. Short of threatening to murder him, there isn't anything that will make him sign it over until we have evidence to charge him and that is taking time."

"Look, she'll get over the cabin. You just have to remind her you love her, and she'll forgive you."

That surprised the hell out of Kade. "I was hoping you'd say that." He reached into his pocket and pulled out a box, placing it on the table in front of Tom. "Open it."

Tom met his gaze for several moments before setting his

Coke bottle on the table and picking up the box. After another glance at Kade, he lifted the lid.

A large princess-cut diamond set in a rose-gold band sparkled in a plush bed of satin. A matching rose-gold chain was threaded through the ring. "As a mechanic she can't wear it at work, so I got the chain so she can hang it around her neck under her work clothes."

Shock shone in Tom's eyes as he looked at Kade. "Good thinking. It's stunning."

Kade smiled. "I bought it the same day I was supposed to secure the cabin for her. I'm just not sure if it's the right time to give it to her. I'm not sure she loves me enough."

"She does," Tom quickly said. "I'm sure of it. But she's not even divorced yet. You can sort of understand why marriage may not be appealing just yet."

"We don't have to get married straight away. I just want her to understand I'm in this for the long haul," Kade said.

Tom shut the box and pushed it over to Kade. "I think deep down she knows that. Tell her what you want."

Kade hesitated, but took the box and put it back in his pocket. "Chance would be a fine thing. She's avoiding me like the plague."

Tom smiled like a sly fox. "I think that's about to change."

"What do you mean?"

"Where do you think Kendra is? I told you I'd help you, and I've got Kendra on the job. She's probably singing your praises right now. She thinks you're the best thing that's happened to Lexie, by the way."

Kade's face broke into a grin. He clunked his beer bottle against Tom's Coke bottle. "Brilliant. And women think they are the romantics."

Chapter Twenty-Four

Kade whistled to himself as he pulled into his garage. If Tom thought he could win Lexie back, the world looked a much brighter place.

Engrossed in his ideas of how to approach Lexie, it took him a minute to note the lights were on in the living room. He walked down the hall towards the lights and slowly pushed open the door. Were the Ericksons after him? *Well, come and get me, you bastards.*

The first thing he saw were rose petals scattered all over his newly laid oak floor.

Not the Ericksons.

A smile formed on his lips. He moved farther into the room, and a pink thong dangled over one of his antique lamps. His smile grew wider while his heart pounded in his chest. He followed the bra and the tank top into the dining room, and the sight before him almost brought him to his knees.

Lying naked on his new dining table was Lexie.

She'd set the table for two. Candles burned at one end, casting soft lighting over every inch of her delectable skin—and sitting atop her stomach were two plates with huge burgers on them.

She looked at him with such love in her eyes, his heart melted. "I hope you're hungry. I made you something special."

His blood started rushing south as he let his eyes travel over the shape of her body, a body he knew intimately. There wasn't an inch of her he wasn't familiar with, any inch he hadn't already worshipped, and he'd never get enough of her.

"Only for you, my love. I'm hungry only for you."

"Then come and get me."

He moved as if in a dream to stand at the edge of the table. He lifted the plates off her and pulled her down the table until her long, sexy legs hung over the edge and he stood between them.

She looked up at him with tears in her eyes. "I'm so sorry if I let you think I didn't love you. I do. So much. It's just—"

"Ssh. I know. Let's forgive each other and simply get on with the loving."

"You've done nothing that needs forgiving, unlike me." Caressing his jaw, Lexie said, "I love *you*."

He smiled and removed his shirt, ripping the buttons as he was in such a rush. "I've missed you so much."

She sat up and began undoing the buttons on his jeans. "I've missed you more."

Kade brushed her hands away in impatience. "I doubt that. You mean everything to me."

Drawing back, Lexie gazed into his eyes. "You mean more to me than a cabin. I'm sorry it took me so long to understand that."

He freed himself from his briefs. "Let's talk later. I'm hungry —for you." He set about feasting on his beautiful lady, his soul filled with such happiness he wondered if this was a dream.

S uccess! Her plan worked. But all thoughts of victory fled as Kade leaned forward and touched her with his tongue, just lightly caressing. Her body recognized the sensation, and she pushed her hips forward, begging for more.

His hands encircled her buttocks, pulling her down and then upwards to give his mouth better access. Kade knew exactly where and how to touch her to prolong her pleasure. She'd never, ever felt anything like it, and she was sure she was about to faint from the heightened sensations sweeping over her.

Her breathing grew ragged. She no longer cared that the table was cold and hard against her back. She wriggled closer, urging him on. His tongue stabbed deep within her, making her shudder. Her head lolled from side to side. Her flesh seemed to burn; a heat consuming her from the inside.

It was almost too much to endure, yet she prayed he'd never stop. Her eyes widened in anticipation of what was yet to come —then she closed them tightly as her climax ripped through her.

His tongue lapped at her, making it last, drawing out each shuddering sensation until she was so satiated, she couldn't move.

Before she could gather herself together, he stood over her and took her mouth in a deep, searching kiss. His tongue swept in so she could taste herself. Her arms crept around his neck, and he pulled her close to him.

"God, you're addictive. I want you more than I've ever wanted any other woman. The taste of you drives me wild. I'll never have enough of you."

He couldn't wait any longer so he used his thighs to part hers wider and pressed his aching cock into her, savoring her tightness as, inch by inch, he slowly entered until he had filled her to the hilt.

Her eyes rolled back and she let out a deeply satisfied sigh. "I love having you deep inside me."

Gratified by her response, his body rejoiced at the hotly

arousing sight of her beneath him. He held himself still above her, his arms shaking. He wanted to pound into her, but knew if he did so, he wouldn't last.

When he refused to move, she opened her eyes. "We have all night, Kade. Hell, we have forever."

She was a prize, all right. God almighty, she was tight and fiery around his cock. She punctuated her words by arching her body, forcing him to withdraw and then sink back into her, penetrating her deeper. As she moved, he looked down, and the sight of his erection coated with her juices increased his own craving until he couldn't deny her anymore. At this rate, she would make him come faster than a schoolboy.

He used his hands to steady her hips so he could thrust in more deeply. He pushed her legs up higher, opening her fully, and at last his control evaporated. As if on the edge of insanity, he pounded into her hot depths. She tilted her hips, matching him thrust for thrust, her bountiful breasts jiggling enticingly as he slammed into her. He could feel his balls become tight and full as they brushed against her. He would not last…

A sharp cry broke from her lips as her fingernails dug deep into his buttocks, and her tight sheath contracted around him with spasms of pleasure, her breath coming in loud gasps.

As she continued to contract around him, the tightness drew out his own release. With a roar, he thrust one final time and climaxed. He collapsed on top of her, completely spent, unable to hold himself up any longer. His body throbbed with pleasure.

He drank in big gulps of air, enjoying the feel of the slowly ebbing waves of their climax.

"I love you so much, Kade." Her soft words were the greatest gift she could give him.

"I love you, too, Lex. What do you say we move you in tonight?"

"Wow. You're in a rush."

Cupping her face, Kade said, "I've been going crazy without you, and I don't want to be apart from you one more night."

"I think that sounds like a fabulous plan. Let's spend the weekend moving me in and making love in every room of this very large, beautiful house."

He pulled her off the table, and they both laughed as they saw the burgers and plates on the floor.

"I hope you didn't spend too much time making those."

"Nope, it was more about getting the bedroom ready, and the petals."

He scooped her into his arms. "Bedroom? That sounds intriguing. Dinner can wait."

"But I can't."

He kissed her soundly. "Your wish is my command." And he carried her upstairs to their bedroom, where he spent the night showing her how much he loved her.

The next morning, Lexi woke to find Kade sleeping soundly beside her, and happiness surged. Last night she'd thought she'd die from pleasure. Never had she been loved so thoroughly.

She lay back, soaking in the delicious Kade, marveling at how handsome he was. How had she gotten so lucky? It was about time, really. But as usual, she wondered what else could go wrong. Life usually sent her a curve ball just as good things happened.

She pushed her insecurities away. Kade loved her. She'd believe in that.

She quietly slipped out of bed and quickly showered and dressed. Today she was moving in with the man she loved. Nothing would destroy the happiness of this moment.

She wanted to make him breakfast and tidy up downstairs

before he woke. She walked into the dining room and smiled at the memory of last night. She picked up all the mess, and soon she had the plates cleared and the table sparkling clean.

Finally, she picked up Kade's discarded shirt and jeans, and something fell out of a pocket.

She stood staring at the little blue box as it lay on the floor, and she froze. *Did she want to know?*

Of course she did.

She bent and picked up the box. Easing up the lid, and a gasp escaped.

The diamond ring was so beautiful. Had he bought it for her? When?

She heard Kade coming down the stairs and quickly slipped it back into his pocket and placed his folded clothes on the chair, before heading into the kitchen to make omelets for them both.

Or *try* to make omelets. She tingled all over, not sure what her response would be if he asked her. Her divorced wasn't final, and it was too soon to think about marrying again. Or was it?

She felt his body heat as he slid his arms around her, pressing a kiss to her neck. "You should have woken me. I would have helped clean up since I contributed to the mess."

"You earned a sleep-in. Besides, I want to impress you with my cleaning skills since my cooking skills suck."

He moved round her. "Then I'll make breakfast. Can you make coffee?"

"That I can do."

They bustled along nicely and soon they were back at the dining table, but eating off it this time. They'd barely started when the doorbell rang, and in walked Jason.

Lexie hadn't seen him for a week, but he looked well.

"Sorry if I'm intruding." Kade shook his head and beckoned him forward. "I'm all moved into the guesthouse," Lexie threw a look at Kade. "And I've brought the divorce papers, all signed."

"You signed them?" Lexie asked, amazed.

"Yeah. Sorry it took me so long, but I had to get my head on straight." He took a seat at the table. "I'm sorry I put you through so much, and really, I'm happy for you and Kade. I'm looking forward to starting over and earning forgiveness. I know I have a long haul in front of me, and I'm hoping we can all get along, because I'll need all the help I can get from my family and friends."

"Thank you, Jason." And she meant it. "It's good to see you looking so well." She reached for Kade's hand. "We're always here if you need us."

"I know. You look good together."

This was awkward. It was obvious she'd spent the night with his brother. She couldn't help feeling a tad uncomfortable.

"Would you like some breakfast? There are plenty of omelets to go around." When Jason nodded, Kade rose to get him a plate and some coffee.

"I also have something else for you," Kade heard him say to Lexie as he entered the kitchen.

Then he heard Lexie cry out, and he rushed back. "What did he do? Are you all right?"

Lexi looked up at him, tears welling in her eyes. "He's given me the deed to my cabin. I own it again!"

"Well, technically, Kade's given the deed to the cabin back to you. I used his money. Well, I gave Mrs. Erickson my word that Kade would pay her for the cabin, actually."

Lexie was out of her chair and hugging Jason.

"How the hell did that happen?"

"When I heard your story about Charlie and Jack, and what they were doing, I knew Mrs. Erickson would have no idea. Her husband built that racing team, and she'd be appalled at what her sons were up to. If they get caught, it would destroy the family business. So I told her everything. She agreed to sell the cabin back as long as you kill the story. She's promised to stop their illegal activity. And she's hired a me to head the parts division to ensure that happens."

Kade sighed. "You had no right to make that deal. It's my story."

At Kade's words, Lexie said, "Come on, Kade. You bought a wreck and spent a fortune getting me to restore it, only to ensure I didn't press charges against Jason. Mrs. Erickson is only asking for the same chance to keep her sons out of jail and her business intact."

Lexie's words tore at him. Jason's offending was not at the same level, or was it? It was to Lexie.

"You did that for me?" Jason asked.

"Well, I had an ulterior motive. I had the hots for Lexie."

The three of them burst out laughing, and suddenly the awkwardness vanished.

"I'm moving in with the man I love, Jason is looking healthy *and* he has a new job, and I get my cabin back, all on the same day. Who would have believed it?" She beamed a smile at them both. "Life couldn't get any better."

Kade knew it could. He saw the outline of the box in the pocket of his folded jeans. Now was not the time to propose. It was too soon, and Jason was here. He'd ask her later. Once she was all moved in.

Chapter Twenty-Five

Stella and Kendra were busy helping her pack and load her Jeep with her few possessions.

"I'm so happy for you, Kade's an awesome guy."

Stella's words sounded wistful, and when Kendra left to carry another box to the Jeep, she had to ask. "What's going on between you and Marcus?" At Stella's silence, Lexie added, "I saw you coming out of Bad Boy Autos one night, and you were kissing. It looked like you two were an old married couple."

Stella's eyes welled. "I wish."

Lexie rocked back on her haunches, the book she was about to place in a box forgotten. "What?"

Stella angrily brushed the tears from her face. "I've stupidly fallen in love with Marcus. Please don't tell Kendra, she'd try to get involved and it will only make everything worse."

"When did this happen? I *thought* you acted strange at Kendra and Tom's wedding. You grilled me as to whether I'd ever had a thing with Marcus."

Stella plonked down on the floor. "I've never been a woman who wanted marriage and kids. My father is on wife number five so the idea of what many see as a disposal piece of paper wasn't important to me. I loved playing the field, and Marcus was one of my friends with benefits. Then Connor came along, and I saw Tom and Kendra with their son, and suddenly, as if a bomb went off, I knew I wanted that too. With Marcus. My clock is ticking."

The words "bad choice in men" kept echoing in Lexie's head.

"But you know Marcus. He doesn't want to be tied down, and he's shown no desire for kids."

"So what are you going to do?"

Stella began repacking a box. "Nothing. What can I do? I tried pulling back, and I hoped he'd miss me, but I'm not sure he notices me unless I'm in his face." She gave Lexie a sad smile. "Do you think you'll ever get married again?"

Lexie opened her mouth, but no words came out.

"Don't know, huh?" Stella said for her.

"Don't know what?" Kendra asked as she came through the door.

"If I'd marry Kade."

Kendra did a little dance. "So he's asked you already!"

Lexie jumped to her feet. "Oh, no. No, he hasn't... but I found the most gorgeous ring in his pocket."

"Do you want him to ask?" Stella asked, looking up from the floor.

Lexie's heart pounded in her chest and her mouth went dry. She didn't know.

Kendra walked forward and hugged her. "I guess not. You'd immediately know if you did. Give it time. You'll know when it's right."

She hugged Kendra back. "I'm so happy just to be moving in with him. I love Kade. And I know we can be happy. I don't need a ring to tell me that." She bent and taped up the box she'd just finished packing. "Come on. This is the last of it. The boys will be arriving soon to collect the furniture. I'm donating it to Pastor Sal's mission."

Happiness suffused her heart, and even though she wasn't ready to marry Kade, that didn't mean she wouldn't be ready in the future. But for now, she was thrilled about moving in with him. To be starting a new life and journey with a man who loved her.

After one last look at the place where she'd licked her wounds, she shut the door, ending the worst period of her life, and jumped in her Jeep to drive back to the man she loved with every particle of her being, anxious to begin the next chapter of their lives together.

Epilogue

"**D**o you think she'll ever marry him?" Lexie heard Zip ask Sully a few months after she'd moved in with Kade.

The gang was enjoying Friday evening together at Sully's place. Some of his other friends were there, and the two crowds mixed and mingled well since most of them were part of the racing scene.

She and Kade sat at a long picnic table, a huge striped umbrella shading them. They were drying off after swimming and playing in the pool.

"I don't know, Zip. I wouldn't rule it out," Sully said.

Lexie tried to hide a smile as she looked up at Kade. His eyes shone with restrained laughter, indicating he was eavesdropping, too.

"I hope so. They're a great couple. Lexie deserves happiness."

Kade leaned down and whispered, "I agree."

Lexie barely held in a laugh.

"That may be, but I hope they don't rush into it. Lex has been through enough hell. I think Kade's a good guy, but if he breaks her heart, I'll punch him in the head."

Lexie felt Kade tense at Marcus' remark, and she put a hand on his thigh, holding him in place.

"Since when did you become so protective of her?" Sully asked. "I thought you hated her?"

"Yeah, well, we've talked over some stuff, and I think we've come to an understanding. Besides, we were both screwed over by Jason Colter," Marcus replied. "It's bonded us."

Lexie muffled a snort, and Kade chuckled quietly.

"You guys are worse than a bunch of nosey old ladies at bingo," Kendra remarked, drawing laughs from the men. "Don't you have better things to do than speculate about other people's business?"

"Not really," Marcus replied. "Then again, we could talk about how you're knocked up again already. Yeah, that's a great topic."

"Shut up, Marcus," Stella said.

Lexie hated seeing the pain in her friend's eyes... but she would talk to Stella tomorrow. Marcus definitely hadn't liked it when earlier, one of Sully's friends took a shine to Stella and was openly flirting with her. Perhaps there was hope.

"Don't get me wrong; I love being an uncle, but you and Tom are giving bunnies a run for their money."

"You love spoiling my kids, and it doesn't look like you'll have any of your own soon, so stop complaining."

At Kendra's taunt, Marcus yelled across the backyard, "Hey, Tom! How about you stay off your wife once in a while, huh? Maybe let her rest a little longer between kids?"

Tom was in the pool playing volleyball with some people. He turned at Marcus' yell and gave him a toothy grin. "For the record, you got that backwards, bro, but piss off anyway."

Everyone, including Kade and Lexie, cracked up.

"I hate you guys," Kendra said and came to sit with Kade and Lexie. "I like the company over here much better."

"Glad to have you," Lexie said.

She smiled at them with a speculative gleam in her eyes that matched her brother's. Kendra had a softer personality than Marcus, but in truth, she was no less nosey.

"So, any babies in your future, guys?"

Kade held his hand over Lexie's head and pointed down at her. "Ask this one. She's in charge of that department."

Lexie gasped and punched his thigh. "We've *both* decided that right now isn't a good time. You have a new book contract, and have written shit bugger all, and I'm swamped at work. Getting pregnant now isn't a good idea. Besides, we're not even married yet."

Kendra pounced. "Yet? *Yet*? Does that mean you're engaged?" She turned to Kade. "Did you ask her again?" Back to Lexie. "Did you say yes?"

Lexie heard a flurry of activity behind her and Kade, and Marcus and company swooped down on them, joining them at the table. All eyes turned on the couple, waiting for their answer.

They looked at each other, and Lexie's mouth turned down. "Sorry, guys."

Expressions of disappointment surrounded them, and even Sully looked a little disappointed. Kade and Lexie laughed at their prodding to "do the deed," as Sully put it. Kendra admonished him, and the siblings started a mouth-battle that ended up in a challenge to a game of volleyball.

Once the furor had died down, Kade put an arm around Lexie. "How do you feel about going home and putting steaks on the grill? Maybe drinking a little wine?"

"I think that's a fine idea."

They made the rounds, saying goodbye to their friends, and walked to the Alfa. Kade only drove it on the weekends or for special occasions.

He threw the keys to Lexie. "Your turn."

Lexie caught them, unlocked the door, and slid behind the wheel. She turned the ignition and smiled at the growl of the engine before it turned into a soft purr. It reminded her of the throaty purr her man made in their bed. Seatbelts on, Lexie headed for home. She loved that word. The house she shared with Kade was a home. A place where they came together and shared their lives.

Opening the glove compartment, Kade took out the blue box containing Lexie's engagement ring and opened it.

It was on a beautiful gold chain, because a mechanic couldn't work with a rock that size on her finger. As he slipped the chain over her head, she asked, "When are we going to put them out of their misery?"

A devilish smile curved Kade's mouth. "When their reaction stops being funny." He sobered and arched an eyebrow. "Unless you're saying that you're ready to let everyone know?"

Lexie watched him straighten the chain, making sure the ring hung straight. It was amusing and touching how fussy he was about it. Her eyes traveled up his chiseled torso, and over his wide shoulders before meeting his gaze. "Not tonight. Tomorrow is soon enough. Let's go home and celebrate."

His grin never ceased to make her heart beat a little faster. "Again?"

She leaned over and pressed a kiss to his mouth. "And again, and again," she whispered against his lips.

Kade tried to claim her lips, but she laughed and moved out of reach. "Safety first, I'm driving."

"Tease," he accused.

She winked at him. "Just a little preview of what comes after dinner."

Kade groaned. "After dinner? You're killing me here, and you know it."

"Patience is a virtue, Kade."

"Screw patience."

They hit the freeway, and Lexie downshifted. "You're right. Patience is overrated." She pressed down on the accelerator, shifted and sent them flying along the road.

Kade whooped, and she joined him as they sped toward the darkening horizon. The motor roared, and she thrilled to the sound, her heart hammering almost as hard as it did when she made love with Kade.

Looking across the car at the man who seemed to have endless patience, Lexie's heart flooded with emotion as he grinned back at her. Every day she woke up, she fell a little more in love with him. How could she keep refusing his daily proposals when he'd repeatedly proven himself to her?

She'd accepted his proposal the weekend she'd taken him to the cabin and shared her memories of her mother with him. He'd gotten down on one knee at the lake front where she'd sprinkled her mother's ashes, and promised they'd make memories at the cabin of their own, and they had.

The ring around her neck clunked against the locket she held so dear. Her mother was always with her, and it was as if her mother was saying, "Well done, my girl. Be happy." And she was.

The happiness they now shared had been a long time coming, but their slow ride had been just what she'd needed. It amazed her how understanding Kade had been about it, how wonderfully he treated her.

She turned back to the road and felt his hand slid under the back of her hair. He gave her neck a little squeeze, and that little gesture was so filled with love that it almost brought tears to her eyes.

"Step on it, babe. I'm hungry."

Glancing at him, she knew by his expression that he wasn't talking about food. Her appetite had suddenly taken the same direction, and she decided that steak would have to wait. "Tighten your seat belt, sexy."

With practiced ease, Lexie sent the car sailing and weaved between the cars ahead. Just like they were flying along now, she didn't need a slow ride anymore. She was ready to leave all the heartache and sorrow behind and race into an incredible future, with the man she loved by her side.

THE END

Click here to read a snippet from Reckless Curves - Drive Me Wild book #1

Click here to sign up to Bron's Book Club newsletter and receive your FREE eBook.

Read other books by Bronwen Evans

Make sure to check out these titles and more on Bron's website.

A Snippet From LOVE ME - Coopers Creek book #1

The first book in *USA Today* bestselling author, Bronwen Evans's flirty new contemporary romance series... Love Me is an enemies to lovers, second chance romance story.

Emily Stanford's trip to New York, and her plan to bring her orphaned goddaughter home to Coopers Creek, backfires. Hayley's coming home but to Emily's horror she's hired as Hayley's nanny and moving in with her ex-lover, Hayley's uncle, the handsome cowboy come banker, Tyler Jeffries. He still makes her heart pound-even though four years ago he walked away from their relationship without a backward glance.

Tyler hates that he has no choice but to let Emily move in, but this is about Hayley and what she needs. He can't believe the woman he blames for his sister's death still fiercely fires his blood. Back in Coopers Creek, out of his comfort zone, coping with PTA meetings and white picket fences, he lets his heart's defenses down, only to have Emily betray him again...

Coopers Creek holds painful memories for Emily and Tyler. Can they forgive each other; can the town hold a beautiful new future for them both?

Chapter One

Tyler Jefferies had ridden rampaging bulls, with horns long enough to gore vital organs, and bucking stallions, whose kicks could've left him permanently singing soprano, but the little girl crying in front of him was more terrifying than any beast he'd ever faced. He found himself momentarily helpless in the face of her sorrow, with absolutely no clue how the hell to handle the situation.

His seven-year-old niece, Hayley, looked up at him with misery shining in her big blue eyes. In that moment, she looked so much like her mother, Lizzie, that pain ripped through him. Tyler had thought the anguish of Lizzie's death would lessen over time, but he still missed his little sister as much as ever. He'd lost a big part of himself the day she'd died.

Then four weeks ago, his mother, Maggie Jeffries, had also passed away, leaving Tyler to raise this sad and frightened child on his own. And it scared him to death. He was supposed to have looked after Lizzie and had horribly failed her.

Here he was, a wealthy, powerful investment broker who'd faced and ruthlessly conquered many formidable opponents, yet one tiny girl had the power to bring him to his knees.

"I made a mess."

"I see that, sweetheart."

It came to him in a flash of insight—he needed a nanny. He knew nothing about raising kids. As he gazed at his seven-year-old niece, he told himself to man up. He needed to make sure that she was properly cared for. Life had dealt Hayley some very cruel hands.

Right after she'd turned three, she'd lost Lizzie, and now

Tyler's mother was gone, the only mother that Hayley had ever really known. Too many people had been taken from her. The agony of such loss was written on her little face and Tyler would do anything to erase it.

"I'm sorry, Uncle Ty."

He looked at the carton of milk lying on its side on the kitchen floor, from which milk dripped and spread across the very expensive limestone tile.

Picking Hayley up, he grabbed a dishcloth, and wiped milk off her little pink sneakers before carrying her upstairs.

"It's okay, honey. It was just an accident. You know what they say, no use crying over spilt milk."

Hayley smiled faintly at his lame joke and Tyler felt proud that he'd made her feel a little better.

"It's been a long day. Why don't you get ready for bed, and then I'll come read you a story?"

"Any story I want?"

"Yeah. Any one you want," he replied, hugging Hayley closer.

Her tiny arms wound tighter around his neck. "You won't leave me, will you? I'll be all alone if you do."

Her words cleaved him in two. She'd been clingy ever since he'd brought her to New York City three weeks ago. It was so different from her home in the backwater town of Cooper's Creek, near Denver, Colorado. Already struggling with her loss, Hayley was having a hard time making the transition from country life to big city living.

Her world now revolved around Tyler, her only living relative. She panicked if he wasn't around, if he got home late, or if he didn't call her at least once a day. He couldn't blame her. What kid in her situation wouldn't be scared to death?

"I'll never leave you, Hayley. We're a team now, and teams stick together."

Hayley was quiet for a moment before softly asking, "Can

Aunt Emily come and visit me? I miss her…" She dissolved into tears against his shoulder.

Tyler closed his eyes against the pain lancing through him. "She's not really your aunt, sweetheart."

"She's my godmother. Nana told me that she's my back-up mommy. She was Mommy's best friend. I miss her, Uncle Ty. I miss Cooper's Creek and my friends. I wanna go home!" she cried as she clung to him.

Tyler's throat constricted and he couldn't answer. Guilt ravaged him. He knew Hayley wasn't happy in New York, but what could he do? This was where he lived and worked. He needed to find a solution—and soon. He hadn't protected Lizzie when it had counted, but he'd damn well protect Hayley.

She wanted Emily.

Emily. He didn't want to think about Emily. Until three weeks ago, when he'd had to face her over his mother's coffin, he hadn't seen Emily since his sister's funeral four years prior. But she still filled his dreams and he hated his renewed weakness for her. He vowed to put her out of his head. He'd done it once before and he could do it again.

Tyler lowered Hayley unto her bed. "I'll be up soon. I just have to talk with Allison."

He watched with a breaking heart as Hayley slid off the bed and slowly walked with downcast eyes into her bathroom.

Tyler sighed and went back downstairs to take care of the mess in the kitchen, but Allison, his elderly housekeeper and temporary nanny, had already beaten him to cleaning up the spilt milk.

"I'm sorry about that, Allison."

"Hey, accidents happen."

He gave her a bland smile as he ran a hand through his black hair. "Thank you for agreeing to move in and watch Hayley until I find a replacement. I have no idea how long that will take. I've had trouble finding anyone suitable."

"Well, you've only got another week before I leave on my cruise." She wrung out the cloth over the sink. "I fed her at six. There's some food in the fridge. I wasn't sure if you'd be hungry."

"Thanks." He had no appetite.

"Oh, by the way, a woman dropped by this afternoon. Said she was a friend of your sister's and wanted to see how Hayley was," Allison said. "I told her Hayley was at dance class. She left her cell number and the name of the hotel where she's staying. She wants you to call her."

Tyler's breath caught in his throat. *She wouldn't dare.* Casually, so he didn't convey the sudden tension in his body, he asked, "Did she leave a name?"

Allison nodded. "Emily Stanford."

Painful memories warred with erotic images of a sexy blonde rolling around naked in his bed. Images from four years ago that still burned in his mind.

Guilt swamped him as it always did when he thought of Emily, his younger sister's best friend. Lizzie…a single mother at eighteen, dead at twenty-one, she'd been wild and uncontrollable. But he should've tried harder to reach her. Being three years her senior, he should've taken his role as her big brother and protector more seriously. If he had, she might be alive today.

He would always blame himself—and Emily.

Blame her for distracting him, and worse, for covering for Lizzie. That night, Emily had said she loved him yet she betrayed him in the same breath. If only she'd told him what Lizzie had been up to that night, Lizzie would be alive today, and Hayley would still have a mother.

Tyler would never forgive Emily. His fist tightened around the piece of paper, crushing the note Allison handed him into a ball before shoving it into the pocket of his navy blue suit jacket. He'd call Emily when hell froze over.

His cellphone rang. He pulled it from his pocket and looked at the number lighting the screen. He silenced the call from his latest lover with a heavy sigh.

Allison raised an eyebrow. "I'm here. You haven't been out for almost four weeks. That's not healthy for a handsome young man like you."

He bent and placed a kiss on his elderly housekeeper's forehead. "What would you know about handsome men like me?" he teased.

"I was young once, you know. And I know *you*. I've found enough women's lingerie left around here to open a Victoria's Secret store." Her raised eyebrow and waggled finger told him what she thought about his lifestyle.

Tyler began pulling his tie from around his neck as he made for the stairs of his Central Park penthouse apartment. "I'll read to Hayley first, and then maybe I'll go out if you don't mind." He hesitated at the bottom of the stairs.

"Be happy to."

"Thank you."

"No thanks necessary. You've done a lot for me over the last few years."

"You're sure I can't persuade you to stay on? I'll double your salary. I mean it. I'm that desperate."

The smile left Allison's face. "I wish I could, but my husband and I have our trip planned. At our age, you can't take anything for granted. It's our time now."

"What about when you get back? I'll find a bigger place, and you and your husband could move in with us."

"But we'll be away for an entire year on our world trip. You need someone *now*, so you better get on it. I'm sure you'll find the right person. Or better yet, you might meet a nice lady and settle down."

Tyler laughed. "Why is it that women always push men to get married? I'm perfectly happy on my own." He grinned. "I'm not lacking for female company."

"But Hayley is. Your priorities have changed now, Tyler," said the no-nonsense housekeeper. "Besides, wouldn't it be nice to give her a cousin to play with?"

Her words drew him up short. He tried to imagine what his childhood would've been like without Lizzie in it. And God knew how lonely he'd been since she'd been gone. He didn't want Hayley to be lonely, but have his own children?

Having a family wasn't in any of his plans for the future. His corporation, Horizon Enterprises, and making money, were both his baby and his mistress. He loved the rush of the deal almost as much as he loved sex, and he was equally skilled at both.

He knew what family meant. Responsibilities. At fifteen his father had left and Tyler had to step up. He didn't resent the fact he'd had to take charge but he wasn't in a hurry to be responsible for others again. Lizzie's death under his care taught him a lesson he'd never forget.

Alison interrupted his musings. "Well, I can see I've given you enough food for thought. Go read to Hayley and then go have some fun. You need to blow off some steam."

"Okay. Thanks again." As he went upstairs to his warm bundle of responsibility who waited for her story, he thought that blowing off steam was definitely in order.

Thinking about the women that the employment agency had sent filled him with dismay. The first four he'd interviewed had immediately been rejected by his niece. It had pained him to decline number three, a sexy brunette with breasts the size of ripe melons, but he'd realized that sleeping with the help wasn't a good idea.

He hadn't been sure he'd be able to resist the temptation. He also didn't want Hayley to get used to a woman he'd soon tire of and let go. His rule of thumb was to keep his relationships brief and casual so no one got hurt. He never wanted to endure that kind of torture again.

Later, as he stood under the shower spray, after having read to Hayley until she'd fallen asleep, he thought about the woman who visited his dreams far too often of late. The image of Emily naked as she swam at their favorite watering hole slipped into his brain.

Tyler genuinely liked women and loved sex. Always the considerate lover, he enjoyed giving as much pleasure as he received. There was nothing better than feeling a woman come alive, surrendering herself under his talented hands and mouth.

But Emily was the one woman he'd never stopped craving. Even now, his body hardened as memories of what it had felt like to have her slim legs wrapped around him as he'd sunk deep into her slick heat. *Christ.* His hand strayed lower over his tight groin. Maybe he should take the edge off before he went out tonight. He was a cocked gun, primed and ready to go off.

No. He'd been doing too much of that lately. *Damn you, Emily.* He'd thought he'd crushed her memory under the weight of her betrayal. He turned the shower jet on cold to cool his over-heated body, but it didn't work very well.

Thirty minutes later, the memory of Emily's gorgeous face and the pleasure they'd once shared were still with Tyler as he drove his silver Porsche through the city streets. He wished the memory of her taste, touch and scent no longer haunted him. But, more than anyone, he knew you didn't get anything by wishing, only by taking action.

When he'd left his apartment, he'd been determined that at least for tonight, the woman who'd ripped his heart from his chest would be vanquished from his mind in another woman's bed. So why was his Porsche heading downtown, when his current lover lived uptown?

Want to read more?

BUY links

About the Author

USA Today bestselling author, Bronwen Evans grew up loving books. She writes both historical and contemporary sexy romances for the modern woman who likes intelligent, spirited heroines, and compassionate alpha heroes. Evans is a three-time winner of the RomCon Readers' Crown and has been nominated for an *RT* Reviewers' Choice Award. She lives in Hawkes Bay, New Zealand with her dogs, Brandy and Duke.

www.bronwenevans.com

Afterword

If you'd like to support Bronwen Evans's work here's how you can help:

(ps: Bronwen also has Bron's Bold Belles. Want to learn how you can become part of her team and win a trip to New Zealand to meet her, click here...)

1. Loan this book to your friends.

2. Buy Bron's next book during the first week of release. Sign up for her newsletter (and receive a FREE eBook) so you'll be in the know.

3. Tweet/Share that you finished this book and consider sharing a link to Bron's website.

4. Mention the book on blogs that ask what you're reading. If you discover Bron is blogging someplace, be sure to pop by and leave a comment.

5. Visit and like Bron's Facebook page.

6. Or simply send Bron an email bronwen@bronwenevans.com

Also by Bronwen Evans

Historical Romances

Wicked Wagers

To Dare the Duke of Dangerfield – book #1

To Wager the Marquis of Wolverstone – book #2

To Challenge the Earl of Cravenswood - book #3

Wicked Wagers, The Complete Trilogy Boxed Set

The Disgraced Lords

A Kiss of Lies – Jan 2014

A Promise of More – April 2014

A Touch of Passion – April 2015

A Whisper of Desire – Dec 2015

A Taste of Seduction – August 2016

A Night of Forever – October 2016

A Love To Remember – August 2017

A Dream Of Redemption – February 2018

Invitation To Series

Invitation to Ruin

(Winner of RomCon Best Historical 2012, RT Best First Historical 2012 Nominee)

Invitation to Scandal

(TRR Best Historical Nominee 2012)

Invitation to Passion

July 2014

(Winner of RomCon Best Historical 2015)

Invitation To Pleasure

Novella February 2020

Imperfect Lords Series

Addicted to the Duke – March 2018

Drawn To the Marquess – September 2018

Attracted To The Earl – February 2019

Contemporaries

The Reluctant Wife

(Winner of RomCon Best Short Contemporary 2014)

Coopers Creek

Love Me – book #1

Heal Me – Book #2

Want Me – book #3

Need Me – book #4

Drive Me Wild

Reckless Curves – book #1

Purr For Me – book#2

Other Books

Dukes By The Dozen Anthology Boxed Set

Christmas In Kilts Anthology Boxed Set

Highland Wishes And Dreams